I0726908

RONALD,

THE BOY WHO WAS ALLERGIC TO EVERYTHING

GARY ARMS

ALL RIGHTS RESERVED, NO PART OF THIS PUBLICATION MAY BE EITHER REPRODUCED OR TRANSMITTED BY ANY MEANS WHATSOEVER WITHOUT THE PRIOR PERMISSION OF THE PUBLISHER.

©TEXT GARY ARMS
COVER - PUBLIC DOMAIN IMAGES ANATOLY777
MODIFIED BY DIANE NARRAWAY

EDITED BY GINGER FYRE PRESS
ADDITIONAL EDITING JULIA KRZYZANOWSKA

PUNK WASP PUbLIShING UK

ISBN: 978-1-914071-89-8

MARCH 2023

PUNK WASP PUBLISHING IS AN IMPRINT OF VENEFICIA PUBLICATIONS

ACKNOWLEDGEMENT

Every book stands on top of a mountain of other books.

The mountain for this one includes the descriptions of insects by the entomologist Henri Fabre, Swift's *Gulliver's Travels*, *1001 Arabian Nights Tales*, and Kafka's *Metamorphosis*.

Special thanks to the original "Bubble Boy," David Phillip Vetter, to Evan Schnittman for encouraging me to resurrect an early draft of this novel, to Deborah Duffy Tancrell and Lisa Steinle, and the other friends who read the first chapters of *Ronald*, and to Julia Krzyzanowska and Diane Narraway for their editorial assistance and advice.

 FOR SUSIE

CONTENTS

CHAPTER 1: THE BOY IN THE WINDOW, 1971

"Would you like a story?" Cook said.

For his thirteenth birthday six months ago, Ronald Matthews had received a large, illustrated book titled THE INTELLIGENT BOY'S GUIDE TO INSECTS AND SPIDERS by Dr. Henry Fabber, a present from his father. His father had sent it to him from Ceylon. Or perhaps Brazil. It was hard to keep track of where in the world Mr. Matthews was. He liked to travel.

In his hermetically sealed room, where he was safe, Ronald liked to look at the pictures of the heavily armored insects - each more freakish and frightening than the last - and read the descriptions. He thought he would like to be an insect, especially if his entire body could be housed in a thick, impenetrable exoskeleton and provided with dangerous weapons like horns and stingers.

The book was lying open on a table beside the chair where Cook was sitting. She noticed it and said, "My goodness!"

"Don't be scared, Cook," Ronald said. He found it rather pleasing to think Cook was frightened by the picture—a large, colorful beetle generally found only in tropical regions.

"Scared?" Cook said. "Don't make me laugh. Of a little itty-bitty bug? I'm big, aren't I? Compared to me, that bug is small." Cook shrugged to indicate she did not need to explain what happens when something small and weak is confronted by something huge and mighty.

"It isn't even a bug," Ronald said. "It's a beetle." He had recently learned there was a difference between a bug and a beetle, but he had completely forgotten what it was. He figured Cook would not know either.

"You want to hear the story or not?" Cook said. "It makes no never mind to me."

"Is it about insects?" Ronald said. "I want to hear a story about giant insects. And there must be a boy in it."

"Once upon a time," Cook said, "them insects could talk."

"They could not. How stupid are you? Do bugs have vocal cords? They don't even have tongues! They have tiny itty-bitty brains. They don't have language! When Mom gets home, I'm gonna tell her you are nothing but a big fat liar!"

Cook was a large woman and, when Ronald was feeling weak and disagreeable, he liked to mention her size in hopes it would hurt her feelings. In fact, Cook seemed to be oblivious to such insults. It was hard to be certain, though, because she was wearing protective clothing, including a mask that concealed her mouth and nose.

Cook said, "What happened to this boy was he shrunk."

"That is scientifically impossible," Ronald said. Despite the impossibility of it, he rather liked the idea of a tiny boy. "To what size? Like a dwarf, you mean?"

"Until he was no bigger than one of them talking bugs."

"Wow," Ronald said. "Why would that even happen? What made him shrink like that?"

"My notion is he was a bad boy who sassed the adults. Probably a spell was cast upon him on account of his bad manners. Maybe a curse."

Ronald settled back into his pillows. He loved stories involving curses.

Then he sat up straight. "He would be eaten! He would not survive five minutes! A boy the size of a bug? Something would eat him right up! An ant or a spider, one of the predators. How could he possibly defend himself?"

"I have a notion about that," said Cook.

"About what?"

"The reason them bugs did not gobble him up in nothing flat like you said. It was because he had a condition."

A Boy with a Condition! Who was possibly cursed! Ronald hesitated to say a word for fear Cook might stop telling this story, which in his opinion was becoming terribly intriguing.

"What kind of condition?"

"Poisonous," Cook said. "From head to toe. His blood, his breath. Am I a scientist? I don't know all the details. Them talking insects could smell it on him, the poison. Certain death if they so much as licked him. He could walk around down there in the place where them insects lived and never be harmed. Naturally, he had to hope he would never run into one of them bugs that has a poor sense of smell. A lot of them don't even have noses, do they?" Cook pointed at the photograph of the tropical beetle, which did seem to be lacking any obvious nose. "If you ask me, that boy better watch his step."

Ronald shuddered, thinking about being eaten by a spider with no sense of smell.

"Who put him under the spell? Probably a witch. Or it could have been a wizard. Did he offend a powerful wizard? I bet he did!"

"The boy wakes up. He's wearing his pajamas and lying on his back in what looks like a forest. Except it ain't trees all around him. Everywhere he looks is huge green plants shooting straight up into the sky!"

"Don't tell me. I bet he's in his own back yard."

Cook said. "A normal back yard might seem safe and respectable, a nice place for kids to play, no problem, but once you shrink? Once you're no taller than the average ant? It's a jungle!"

Ronald sighed happily. "How long before he saw his first insect? Was it something huge like a praying mantis? I hope so!"

Ronald Matthews was not a happy child. He could be sweet and pleasant, and everyone agreed he was very bright — for a boy — but he found it impossible to be charming all the time. He often fell into peevish moods. This tendency was not entirely his fault. He had an illness, a condition. The condition meant he had to stay inside.

Margaret Matthews, Ronald's mother, came into his room every night, wearing protective clothing and a mask. The clothing and the mask were not to protect her from him, but to protect him from her. He got sick very easily. Sometimes she told him about her day — her cases, the other lawyers, the accused criminals, the judges, the juries — but her job was time-consuming. She worked long hours on behalf of her accused criminals and often Ronald was already asleep when she peeked into his room.

His most reliable visitor, the person he most often talked to, was Cook.

Cook was not really a cook, at least not professionally; Cook was her last name. She was

Ronald's caretaker. Once upon a time, Cook had worked in a hospital. She had grown old and gotten tired of the aggravation and accepted an easier job, taking care of Ronald. He was her one and only patient. While Ronald's mother was away at her job, Cook cared for Ronald, making his lunch, checking his vital signs, and making sure he took all his medicines at the scheduled times.

While Ronald was finishing his lunch, Cook liked to sit in an armchair in a corner of his room and tell him a story. Ronald felt that he was perhaps getting too old for stories, but the truth was, no matter how irritating and silly Cook was, he enjoyed her stories. They were much more appetizing than her sandwiches. However, his respect for Cook's narrative skills did not prevent him from sometimes accusing her of telling lies or of being shamefully ignorant.

Cook did not seem to mind these accusations. In fact, they seemed to amuse her. When Ronald was accusing her of something or other, she would lean back in her chair. This habit of Cook's, the settling back in her chair, was extremely irritating to Ronald. He could not see her mouth because she was wearing a mask, but he suspected she was smiling at him as if she knew an important secret and he didn't.

Ronald's bedroom window looked out at a field where other children played, boys his age. Ronald had a pair of binoculars, a gift from his far-away father. When he was feeling well, he liked to stand in front of the window and use his binoculars to observe the boys. He had formed strong opinions about them, liking some more than others. Ronald had a hope, which he expressed to no one, that some of these boys would notice him standing there in the window. They would ask each other, "Who is that boy in the window?" Soon, they would be so overcome with curiosity that they would decide to visit him. They would stand out there on the lawn just beyond his window and talk to him. Probably it would be impossible to hear their voices–the window was thick, double-paned, air-tight, impervious to all varieties of dust and pollen — but since they were clever and determined, they would come up with an ingenious solution — perhaps a small chalkboard.

This never happened. Every day, weather permitting, the children played out there in the field, and none of them ever came to visit Ronald.

When the boys came to play in the field, a girl came with them. She never played with the boys, and Ronald wondered if she might be a sister to one of them. Maybe her mom worked all day, and she was not allowed to stay home all by herself. The girl seemed to be ordinary, the usual size and weight, and always carried a big purse with her. The only thing unusual about her was that she had red hair. There was a large tree at one end of the field, the kind of tree with huge spreading branches that provide a lot of shade. The girl pulled a blanket out of her big purse and spread it on the ground. Then she pulled a book out of the purse, lay down on the blanket, and read the book.

Ronald asked Cook to bring him a tablet of paper and a pencil. He was going to write that girl a letter. Over the next two weeks, he wrote twelve letters. Some of them were long and some of them were short. He showed two of the letters to Cook, and she told him he needed to work on his handwriting.

"Do you think girls like letters?" Ronald asked Cook.

Cook said she had no idea.

"I could write her a letter about sports, but I don't know anything about sports. I don't like sports."

Cook said, "If you ask me, what that girl likes is story books."

Every time Ronald wrote a letter, the same thing happened. He would work carefully on it, then he would read it, trying to imagine he was the red-headed girl reading the letter for the first time. Sometimes the letter explained that Ronald was a boy with a condition who could not leave his room. Sometimes it would begin: "I see you like books. I like books too." Some letters began: "I have always loved red hair." After working on the letter for hours, after reading it and reading it again, Ronald would tear the letter into little bits and throw them into his wastepaper basket.

Finally, Ronald decided to write a story. When he finished his story, he tore it out of his notebook, folded it in half, and handed it to Cook. He instructed her to carry the letter to the red-headed girl.

"What girl? All I see is boys."

"Look under that tree, that big tree."

"That girl on a blanket?" Cook unfolded the story. She read the title and the first paragraph of the story. Then she looked at Ronald. "You want me to just hand it to her, no message or nothing? Just say, 'Hey, Ronald wrote you a story. He lives over there in that house, and he has a condition.' If I don't tell her nothing, she'll jump to the conclusion I wrote the story. You don't want that, do you?"

"Do it!" Ronald said. "I don't want you to say ANYTHING. Just give it to her!"

Ronald watched as Cook crossed the field. He was happy to see she had removed her mask and protective clothing, so she looked like a normal person. The boys stopped playing their game to look at Cook. The red-headed girl did not even glance up from the book she was reading until Cook was right there in front of her.

Cook and the girl had a conversation. Ronald watched, using his binoculars. Clearly, Cook was disobeying his instructions and talking to the girl. Unfortunately, Cook had her back to him. Her large body was almost completely blocking his view of the girl.

Cook turned around and came back to the house. Ronald noticed she was no longer carrying the story. He trained his binoculars on the girl. She was putting his story in her purse. She was not even reading it. Two of the boys ran over to talk to the girl. They probably were curious to know what Cook had said. Ronald could see the boys and the girl talking. The girl pointed at her purse. One of the boys, the tall red-haired boy that Ronald thought was the girl's brother, went to the purse and pulled out the story. He was going to rip it up!

The girl jumped to her feet. The boy was grinning and acting as if he was going to tear up Ronald's story. The girl was yelling at him, trying to grab it back. Finally, the boy turned the story into a paper airplane and sailed it at the girl. The story-airplane landed at her feet. So far as Ronald could tell, the story was not seriously injured. The boy and his friend ran back to the field and resumed their game. The red-haired girl sat down on her blanket, still holding the story. She smoothed it out and started reading it.

Ronald sat on the edge of his bed. His heart was racing. He was too excited. He breathed through his mouth. He lay back on his bed and closed his eyes. The important thing when he was in the grip of his condition was to stay calm.

THE POISONOUS BOY
A story by Ronald Matthews

Once upon a time, there was a boy who nobody liked because he was not nice. He said mean things to everyone. He was not even nice to his mother. Or her friend, who happened to be a dangerous wizard. One day, after the boy made a rude comment about the wizard's big nose, the wizard put a curse on him. He made him shrink.

While the boy slept, he shrank until he was no bigger than a flea. A flea is not big. It is smaller than a marble. It is smaller than a pea. The window to his room was wide open. A breeze flew into the room, found the tiny boy, and blew him up to the ceiling, and then down almost to the floor, and finally blew him right out the window. Probably this breeze was a friend of the wizard.

The boy, because of the curse, did not even wake up.

The next morning, when the boy finally did wake up, he was in the world of insects and spiders. OK, it was just his back yard. But it seemed to him a different world. Also, he was still wearing his pajamas.

You may be wondering if he survived even for a minute, even for five seconds. How could a tiny boy like that live? A boy who did not even have an exoskeleton to protect him. Pretty soon he would be discovered by a passing ant, dragged back to the ant nest, and fed to the ant babies. Or something even worse might happen to him.

Fortunately, the wizard had already thought of that problem. He wanted to punish the boy, but not kill him. After all, the boy's mother was the wizard's best friend. He wanted to teach the boy a lesson. He made him poisonous. Every bit of the boy was deadly poison, even his toes, even his ears. The poison had a smell. Ick. A predatory insect might see the boy and want to eat him, but the moment the insect caught a whiff of that poison, the insect would stop in its tracks and change its mind. The only problem was certain insects do not have a sense of smell. One of those might eat him, for example, a spider.

Another problem was the boy did not know all there was to know about insects. He knew a lot because he had read a book called *The Intelligent Boy's Guide to Insects and Spiders* by Dr. Henry Fabber, but he had not read the entire book. He had skipped some of the chapters. Also, even though the guide was helpful, it could not possibly teach a boy everything there is to know about insects. There are so many! According to the guide, there are 350,000 kinds of beetles. And that is just the beetles.

Pretty soon, the boy met his first insect. It was a flea. Fleas do not have wings. All they can do is jump. This particular flea crashed to earth right beside the boy and inspected him.

"You are too small," the flea said. "Do you have any blood at all?" Fleas love blood and will happily bite any mammal. The flea sniffed him. Even though it did not possess a nose, it had the ability to smell things.

"What is that horrible smell? Poison!" And the flea jumped so far and so high, it disappeared into the sky, leaving the boy all alone.

The boy was hungry and wished he could eat breakfast.

Then he met his second insect, a praying mantis. A praying mantis as everyone knows is very big and very dangerous!

If you like this story, I can write you another.

Sincerely,

Ronald Matthews (the Boy in the Window)

CHAPTER 2: THE MOST HORRIBLE INSECT

The next day it rained, so the boys and the red-headed girl did not appear. It rained for three days in a row.

On the fourth day, it was still raining.

When Cook brought Ronald his lunch, she sat down in the armchair and watched him eat his sandwich. "Oh, don't let me forget," Cook said. "You got a letter. I had to put it in the microwave to kill the germs."

Ronald set down his sandwich.

"Not exactly a letter. More like a note. Where'd I put that?"

"Where is it? Give me my letter right now!"

"Don't get yourself into a state. I know I put it somewhere." Cook always wore a white smock. She was exploring its pockets one at a time. "That red-headed girl you like so much brought it back this morning, left it in the mailbox."

Ronald felt his face turn hot. He sat very still for a moment and then took a swallow from his glass of sterilized water. He wanted to scream.

"Here we go!" From a pocket of her coat, Cook pulled out a folded-up piece of notebook paper and handed it to Ronald. "Look on the back."

Ronald unfolded the story, turned it over so he could see the back of the page.

Dear Ronald,

I feel sorry for you and I hope you get stronger. I don't have a condition, but I sunburn real easy so I have to stay out of the sun. Thank you for letting me read your story. My brother read it too. His name is Jim. He has red hair but he's lucky and he never burns. He just gets freckles. My brother likes bugs more than I do. I don't usually like them because they bite and they're ugly. You can write me another story about the Poisonous Boy if you want. My favorite kind of story is horror. Also, I hope your story will include a girl. Not just a boy.

Yours Truly,

Mary Margaret Murphy.

It quit raining. The field beyond Ronald's window dried off, and the boys and the red-headed girl returned.

Ronald worked on his new story for two days. He soon discovered story writing is every bit as difficult as letter writing. His wastepaper basket filled up with the remains of the stories he started and never finished because he hated them. Finally, he asked Cook for help. He felt he could handle the insect characters by himself — with help from Dr. Fabber's *Guide* — but he would like her assistance when it came to writing a horror story, especially one that included a girl. He asked Cook to instruct him in horror stories. "What do they have to contain?"

Cook said, "Monsters of course. And danger! You need plenty of that. And don't forget to include something creepy and weird."

Ronald wondered if maybe Cook could help him with the girl character too. He was fine when all he had to do was write a story about a boy and an insect, especially if it was a praying mantis. An entire chapter of the *Guide* was about mantises. He already had a good explanation of how the boy found himself in the world of insects and spiders — the wizard, the insult to the wizard's nose, and the curse. He even had a decent explanation for why the boy did not get gobbled up immediately by a predatory insect — he was poisonous. But how was he going to get a girl into the story?

Cook said she would think about the girl problem.

"But really, you should solve it yourself. It's YOUR story." Cook suggested Ronald take a nap. She said in her experience the best way to solve a problem is not to think about it. "You'll just give yourself a stomachache if you think too much." She said the best thing to do is fall asleep. "And then, when you wake up, you'll have it, a good idea." Cook adjusted her mask. "I do have a notion though."

"Tell me!" Ronald said.

"The girl in your story? She should have red hair."

Ronald attempted to take a nap, but he found it impossible to fall asleep. He wondered what the boy would eat down there in the world of insects and spiders. Obviously, there would be no one to fix him a sandwich. Where would he get water? And what about the boy's mother? How would she react when she found out her only son was gone, vanished? Would she suspect her friend, the wizard?

While he was thinking about these problems, Ronald fell asleep and dreamed he was the boy in the story.

The boy in Ronald's dream discovered water is easily obtained in the grass forest. In the morning, dew drops are everywhere. Also, there are plenty of puddles, though they tend to be occupied by mosquito larvae. For food, there are fallen apples, sometimes inhabited by hungry worms.

While wandering around in the grass forest, dream-Ronald saw a girl. She had red hair. He only glimpsed her. She was riding on top of a grasshopper. The grasshopper spread its wings and leapt into the air. A wind caught the grasshopper and blew it high up into the sky. Ronald could hear the girl's laugh, a loud happy gurgle that reminded Ronald of his mother's laugh.

When Ronald woke up, he wrote another story.

THE FLY
A story by Ronald Matthews

This story is a horrifying horror story. It includes a monster! It's creepy and weird! Ick! Don't read it if you get scared easy.

Once upon a time, there was a beetle. He had six legs and used them to drag himself around in the grass forest, doing whatever beetles like to do. Mostly they like to eat stuff and get into trouble with the other beetles. This one beetle was acting weird. According to him, he had only five legs.

The other Beetles could see he had six legs, just like everyone else. Beetles can count, but only up to ten. "One, two, three, four, five, SIX!" This is what the other beetles would say when the weird beetle went on and on about how he had only five legs.

The weird beetle said the other beetles were wrong about his legs. One hundred percent wrong. With his antenna, he pointed at one of his legs, which no longer seemed to work properly.

"That one!" said the beetle. "It's not my leg! Cut it off! I don't want it!"

The other beetles decided the weird beetle was crazy.

Pretty soon, the weird beetle was dragging both his hind legs and complaining he had only FOUR legs. According to him, someone, maybe a spider, was attacking him late at night when he was dozing. Beetles sleep but for only half an hour a night, an hour tops. This mysterious attacker was yanking off his legs and attaching other legs – dead ones. The weird beetle figured it was a spider because spiders make sticky web that could be used to glue the fake legs to his exoskeleton.

The other beetles started avoiding the weird beetle.

Eventually, the weird beetle was dragging himself around with just his front pair of legs. His middle pair and his back pair of legs no longer seemed to work. The weird beetle said they were not his legs. "Look at them! Are you blind! Where are MY legs? Someone stole them!"

In the morning, the weird beetle had only one leg that he could still operate. He had five completely useless legs. With his one good leg, the beetle dragged himself in circles. He was so depressed that he did not even complain any more.

That afternoon, the weird beetle died. Probably that was a good thing, said the other beetles.

Then–guess what happened? This is the horrible part of the story. Don't read it, not unless you like to be scared!

The beetle's dead body began to make noises! Grunts! Scratches! Creaking noises–like a rusty hinge on a door. And then a hole appeared in the side of the beetle.

A hole!

It got bigger and bigger until, at last, a worm crawled out, a huge, ugly maggot.

A week before, what happened? A fly, the most horrible of all insects, laid an egg on the exoskeleton of the beetle. The egg hatched and a tiny hungry maggot crawled out, and immediately burrowed under the exoskeleton of the beetle.

The horrible worm lived inside the beetle, eating his insides! It avoided the vital organs of the beetle until the very last. No wonder the beetle's legs did not work! The beetle was not weird! He was being devoured alive! From the inside!

When the hole got big enough, the fat worm crawled out of the dead beetle. It crawled up a stick and turned itself into a pupa. That is what maggots do when they have eaten enough. The pupa hung there, swaying in the breeze, until it cracked open, and a fly climbed out.

The fly wiggled its wings and let its body dry in the breeze! When it was entirely dry, it spread its wings and flew away!

The End.

Ronald showed his story to Cook.
"You think it's horrible enough?"
Cook sniffed.
"You use too many exclamation points."

CHAPTER 3: THE BRAIN SURGEON

Ronald owned a one-volume medical encyclopedia that his father had sent him for a Christmas present. His mother, Mrs. Matthews, was not happy about the present and sometimes threatened to take it away from Ronald because, in her view, reading articles in the encyclopedia just encouraged him to imagine he had illnesses that no normal person had ever heard of. This morning, a Saturday, Ronald was using his encyclopedia to look up perfume allergies.

The previous night, after midnight, smelling of perfume, his mother had entered his room, woken him up, danced around the room, and said she was "very, very happy."

Ronald skimmed the article on perfume sensitivity and told Cook, "I think she may be losing her mind."

"That's one way to describe it," Cook said.

"I may be allergic to perfume. I may have fragrance sensitivity."

"Your mother has a new friend."

Reading from the encyclopedia, Ronald said,

"Symptoms of fragrance sensitivity can include a skin allergy which causes redness, itching, and burning. Runny nose and congestion are also common. Sneezing, headache, even breathing difficulties can also be triggered by strong perfume."

"Oh, for heaven's sake," Cook said. "You don't have any of those symptoms."

"It pays to be cautious," Ronald said. "She reeked!"

"I'm not sure it was perfume," Cook adjusted her mask. "It might have been martinis. She went out dancing with her new friend."

Ronald sniffed. "I think I may have congestion."

Cook said Mrs. Matthews' new friend was a renowned brain surgeon named Dr. Leo Symington.

"We may be seeing more of him, so you better get used to it."

After Cook left, Ronald looked up the word "renowned." It was an adjective that meant "known or talked about by many people, famous." He wondered how his mother would even meet someone like that. Usually, she just knew people like lawyers and accused criminals and judges. He also wondered if he was going to develop a cough. Or even a skin rash.

A week later, Ronald's mother brought home her new friend. Wearing a mask and protective clothing, Dr. Symington made an appearance in the boy's room. Ronald could not see Dr. Symington's face because the brain surgeon was wearing a protective mask, but he could see that the doctor had a broad chest, thick black eyebrows, and was bald. Ronald thought it weird that someone could have furry eyebrows but no hair on top of his head. He noticed the doctor was an inch shorter than his mother and a bit plump. Ronald took an instant dislike to him. He said he had a slight headache and would like to be alone.

Mrs. Matthews said, "Leo, this is my brilliant son, Ronald! Ronald, this is my fiancé, the brilliant Dr. Symington, but you can call him Leo. Isn't that right, Leo?"

The surgeon told Ronald, "You can call me Leo, kid."

Ronald started coughing and said, "I think I'm having a crisis! Call 911! Tell them I may be dying!"

Leo offered to help, after all he was a trained doctor, but Mrs. Matthews said, "I knew this would happen. Ronald, we will come back when you decide to be mature."

Mrs. Matthew and Dr. Symington exited, and Cook came in. She stood in the middle of Ronald's room and did not say anything.

Ronald said, "Quit staring at me! I can't help it if I'm dying!"

Cook checked Ronald's vital signs and told him he was not dying. "I hope you're proud of yourself. You are not running a fever. Your blood pressure is normal, and you only cough when your mom is nearby."

The wedding of Mrs. Matthews and Dr. Symington was covered in the newspaper under the headline:

WEDDING OF THE YEAR!

The article included photos of the happy couple as well as smaller photographs of the mayor, various prominent lawyers, and doctors, and even a picture of a well-known accused criminal.

Ronald felt neglected. Weddings were stupid. Insects don't have weddings, they just mate. Dogs don't have weddings. Birds don't. Humans are the only species that has stupid weddings. Or month-long honeymoons.

He wrote a letter to the red-headed girl and told her he was planning to write a story in which the mother of the Boy Who Shrank is so stupid and gullible that she marries the evil wizard and then gets murdered even though her tiny son tries his best to warn her. He told her that the evil wizard was completely bald and had thick, furry eyebrows just like Dr. Symington. "Plus, he's short!"

Mary Margaret wrote back that he should not be so sensitive. Her parents got divorced when she was six. It wasn't so bad. She lived with her mom and her stepdad and saw her biological dad at holidays.

"I recommend you grow up."

Ronald did not write any more stories for a week. He decided he hated Mary Margaret.

CHAPTER 4: MORE STORIES SOON

Cook told him, "While you were pouting, the red-headed girl knocked on the door. "'Is he dead?'" That's what she asked me. "'Is the poor sick boy dead?'"

"I'm not dead," Ronald said. "Do I look dead? And her name is Mary Margaret. And we are not friends anymore. I hate her!"

Above her mask, Cook's eyes narrowed. She shrugged and looked at her hands which were encased in rubber gloves. "It's no nevermind to me."

"Did she say anything about my story?"

"Where did I put that?"

"She brought it back? That means she read it! Did she write on it? Where is it?"

"I know I put it somewhere."

"Give it to me right now!"

Cook searched the pockets of her smock until she found Ronald's story, the one about the beetle who kept misplacing his legs. "Here it is!"

Ronald rapidly read the note, written in curly girl-handwriting on the back of the page.

Dear Ronald, it's a good story and my favorite kind, horror. I felt sorry for the poor beetle. Also, could your next story have a girl in it? Don't name her Mary Margaret because that would be stupid.

"Go fix me a sandwich," Ronald said. "I need to think."

That afternoon, a sign appeared in Ronald's window. I AM NOT DEAD. MORE STORIES SOON.

Cook said, "I thought you were going to write her a story about a praying mantis. Something cheerful."

Ronald said, "Cheerful?! It's a horror story! Horror stories are not cheerful!"

"I suppose them bugs are religious. It stands to reason. Or else, why would they be called praying mantises?"

"They are not religious! They never pray. It's just the way they hold their forelimbs. It sort of looks like they're praying. But they're not!"

Cook was sitting in the armchair looking at a picture in *The Intelligent Boy's Guide to Insects and Spiders*.

"It says here they're cannibals. The females eat their mates. Ick! They bite their heads off!"

Ronald ignored Cook. He was thinking about the girl. How was he supposed to get a girl into his next story? He decided Cook's suggestion that the girl have red hair was a good one.

Ronald made another decision. It did not seem so much a decision as a discovery. He knew why the girl in the story did not get eaten. It was not because she was poisonous.

"A magic suit," Ronald said.

Cook looked up at him.

"Excuse me, dear, did you say something?"

"The girl wears a suit of invulnerability! She's protected by powerful magic! Nothing can eat her!"

"That's nice. Well, I can't sit here all day listening to your nonsense. Ring the buzzer if you need me, sweetie."

In his notebook Ronald wrote: *The Girl has a sword named Stinger.* He thought Stinger was a good name. Swords, after all, should have names. Ronald wrote:

Dear Mary Margaret, remember how at the end of the first story, the boy met a praying mantis? What happened was the boy was walking through the grass forest, hoping to find something to eat. He was looking both ways, trying to be careful, when he saw a strange plant, tall and green, but did not think anything about it. He was new to the world of bugs and did not yet know that when anything looks the least bit strange, you'd better watch out! The strange plant was in fact a praying mantis. The moment the boy came close enough, the mantis reached out and snatched him!

That would have been the end of the boy except, luckily, praying mantises have a good sense of smell. Most insects do. Some people think because they don't have noses they can't smell, but they can. They smell with their antennae. The praying mantis held the boy with her front legs and sniffed him by waving her antennae over him.

"Yuck!" she said. "What is it? Is it poison?"

"I'm a boy! Please put me down!"

"Nasty, smelly, stinky poison!" said the mantis. She put down the boy. Well actually, she just released him and let him fall to the ground, and then she spread her wings and flew away.

Ronald stared at his notebook. He read over what he had just written. Ronald realized his hero, the boy, was no longer in danger. What good was this story going to be if the mantis just flew away? Everyone knows that the main character in any story should always be in trouble, right up until the end, or else the story gets boring.

What else could the boy do? After the mantis flew away, maybe the boy found a rotten apple and ate a piece of it. Maybe there was a worm in it. That would be cool. The boy and the worm could have a conversation. But how dangerous can an apple-eating worm be? Ronald wrote:

> The next day, the mantis was still hungry. And the boy was distracted. He found a fallen apple and was eating bits of it, talking to the worm inside it, and not paying attention. The mantis sneaked up behind the boy and snatched him.
>
> "I will eat it!" said the hungry mantis. "Even if it is poison! I will take a little bite. A little sample!"
>
> "Put me down!" the boy yelled. "Don't you dare eat me!"
>
> Nearby, the girl on the grasshopper heard the boy. She and her grasshopper were flying – actually, they were gliding on a puff of breeze. She heard the noise and looked down and saw what was happening. The mantis was holding the boy with her forelegs and was considering how best to sample him. Should she nip off a bit of his head or maybe start at the other end with his toes?

The red-headed girl swooped down on her grasshopper and knocked the mantis flying! The boy fell to the ground.

"Jump on!" the girl said. "Hurry!"

The boy climbed up on the back of the grasshopper.

"Thank you, thank you very much for saving me!"

And —

Ronald had no idea what happened next. Did the girl have a home somewhere, a nest? Maybe in a tree? He worried that he really did use too many exclamation points. Probably the girl would smell the poison on the boy. Riding on top of the grasshopper with the boy holding on to her, wouldn't she notice he smelled? Maybe she would dislike the boy as a result. Who likes a stinky, smelly, poisonous boy? Maybe she would order the grasshopper to land somewhere and tell the boy to run away. He would have to fend for himself because she had better things to do than babysit him. Maybe she would tell him to take a bath. Or at least order him to stand downwind.

Ronald sighed. Writing stories was much more difficult than he had thought. He was getting a stomachache. He lay back on his bed and closed his eyes. A minute later, he opened his eyes, sat up, tore his unfinished story out of his notebook, ripped the pages into twenty pieces, and threw them in the wastepaper basket. Then he lay back on his bed and closed his eyes again.

Ronald worked on his new story every day for a week. He was encouraged by the fact that Cook said, every morning, Mary Margaret came to the

door and asked if Ronald had written any more
stories.

A STORY ABOUT A GIRL WITH RED HAIR
by Ronald Matthews

Once upon a time, a girl with red hair
shrank herself until she was no bigger than an
ant. Ants are not big, they are tiny. Her father,
an entomologist, had done it first. An
entomologist is a scientist who studies insects.
Her father was Dr. Henry Fabber, the greatest
entomologist in the entire world. Dr. Fabber
wanted to get to know insects up close and
personal. He didn't want to just collect insects
and dissect them, but to observe them in their
natural habitat and learn all about their
customs and mating rituals. Dr. Fabber's plan
was to shrink himself to ant-size (which is
tiny) and then spend a month in his back yard
studying his beloved insects. When he finished
his studies, he would grow back to his normal
size, call a press conference, and tell the world
about his amazing adventures.

Unfortunately, Dr. Fabber did not
return on the appointed date. Something must
have gone wrong.

The girl decided to search for her dad.

Because she did not want to be eaten,
the girl found a suit of invulnerability so
nothing could eat her, and then shrank
herself.

She had no more than arrived in the
grass forest of her back yard when she realized
she had made a huge mistake.

"Daddy! Where are you?" No one answered. The forest was vast and dark and green and stretched in every direction. How would she ever find her father?

"One cannot take two steps on this dreadful world," the girl said, "without encountering a monster." On all sides, she was surrounded by a forest of grass blades. Beneath her feet were dead stalks, cut off at their base by the lawn service person, pushing a mower big as a mountain range.

Feeling hungry, the girl found a seed, a small one. She gnawed on the end of it and then, thirsty, plunged her head into a dew drop. Delicious. But now she was all wet. She stood in a sunbeam to dry out.

While she was standing there, drying off, she noticed among the blades of grass a tall plant of a type she had never seen before. Wondering if its leaves might be edible, she approached the plant to inspect it.

The moment the girl attempted to touch one of its leaves, the plant reached down and picked her up.

"Hey!" the girl said. "What're you doing?! Put me down!"

The plant held the girl close to itself and examined her with what the girl now realized was a hard, green, pointed head that contained two faceted eyes. The moment it located the girl's head, the plant attempted to bite it off. Finding the girl's head could not be snapped from her neck, it turned her end to end and tried to bite off her left leg. Finding it could not succeed there either, it hummed with frustration.

Congratulating herself for putting on a magic suit that made her invulnerable before shrinking herself and coming to the dangerous world of insects and spiders, the girl told the plant, "You can't eat me. No one can. I'm invulnerable! Put me down this minute."

"Too hard," the plant agreed sadly, but not before it tried to bite off the girl's right leg. It set the girl down on the ground and gazed at her with its head cocked.

"You are not a plant at all. I know what you are," the girl said, "a what-do-you-call-it, a praying mantis."

The elegant creature was thirty feet tall. It moved very slowly and gracefully like an ancient ballerina. And yet, when it grabbed the girl, its arms had leapt through the air as fast as an arrow in flight.

"If it's not rude to ask," the mantis asked, "how long have you lived here among us?'

"It's none of your business, but I just got here. I'm looking for my father."

"Ah," said the Mantis. It lifted its arms into the air, tilted its head, and froze in this position. If the girl had not observed the process with her own eyes, she would have been certain it was a normal green plant with two branches and a soon-to-open bud at the top.

"You look *exactly* like a plant."

"You are too kind." The mantis folded up its serrated arms, each one a killing contraption equipped with dangerous hooks and sharp edges.

"May I ask you a question?"

"Naturally."

"Would you remove your suit?"

"Certainly not!"

"I thought you wouldn't. Such a pity." The Mantis elevated its arms, again transforming into something that resembled a plant.

The End

When this story came back to Ronald, there was a note written at the end in curly handwriting.

"I like this story better than the other two because it's about a girl. I like that she has red hair because I have red hair too. I like the suit of invulnerability but where did she get it? I don't think you can buy them at the store. How would she find something like that? You need a better explanation. You can write me another story if you like, but don't write one about spiders because I hate them. Yours Truly, Mary Margaret."

CHAPTER 5: A SPIDER

Ronald was experimenting with his name. What if he changed it to Donald? Would Donald Matthews be a different sort of boy than Ronald Matthews? Better or worse? Hard to say. What if he shortened his name or made it into something more like a nickname? Ronnie Matthews? Maybe other kids would like him better if he was called Ronnie. Good old Ronnie. Or Ron. Just plain Ron. Everyone likes Just Plain Ron.

Ronald was feeling sad. His mother and Doctor Leo were off honeymooning in India and would be gone for a month. Cook had microwaved the local newspaper to kill off any dangerous germs and brought it to him so he could turn to the Society Page and see the picture of the prominent criminal defense attorney and the renowned brain surgeon visiting the Taj Mahal.

So far, he had received two postcards from the honeymooners. Cook microwaved the postcards before bringing them to him. One was a picture of an elephant standing in the middle of a road. The second one was a picture of a monkey sitting in a tree.

Ronald wished Mary Margaret would come to see him, but you can't very well microwave a girl. Mary Margaret was probably covered in germs.

Ronald studied the chapters in the *Guide* that described spiders. He thought he would write a story about a spider, maybe a wolf spider. What difference did it make if Mary Margaret did not like stories about spiders? Probably other kids would like a story about a spider.

Ronald had looked up the definition of horror and discovered it referred to stories that make the reader look under the bed to be sure nothing scary was lurking down there. A ghoul, a ghost, a demon, a centipede. *Horror stories make you believe your nice safe world is not nice or safe!*

Ronald suspected that probably there was not enough danger in real life for ordinary kids which was why they enjoyed horror stories so much. Ronald felt that HIS world was neither nice nor safe. He looked at the postcards and decided he would write a horror story about a mother, and she would be the kind of mom who would NEVER abandon her kids to go on a honeymoon. And guess what? It would be about a boy! Not a girl. A boy and a spider!

THE SPIDER MOTHER,
a Story by Ron Matthews

One morning, soon after his arrival in the grass forest, the boy discovered a path. Who made it? Where did it lead? While he was walking on this path, feeling safe, an unfortunate thing happened. He stumbled over a sticky rope, and a monster the size of an elephant jumped on top of him.

The boy was stunned and confused, not to mention scared, so he did not have a clear idea of what happened next. A fat brown spider was gripping him firmly with her two forelegs. She wanted to bite him. She wanted to sink her fangs into him, except she did not like his smell.

"Poison!" said the brown spider. She had been waiting beside the path for an entire weekend without capturing any prey, so she didn't want to release the boy, even if he did stink.

"Please, put me down," the boy said. He was recovering his wits. "As you have probably noticed by now, I am FULLY poisonous. Every bit of me is lethal. Best to put me down and let me go about my business."

The spider snorted angrily because she wanted very badly to sink her tusks into the boy. Afraid of the poison he contained, she instead tied him up securely. Using her forelegs and a middle pair of legs, she whirled the boy around and around as if he was a top. While she spun him, a braid of transparent ropes shot out of spigots located at the end of her abdomen. Eventually, the boy was so covered in ropes he looked like a mummy.

Insects have six legs, but spiders are eight-legged arachnids. Holding the mummy against her chest with her forelegs, the spider used her other six legs to run to her nest, which was nearby, carefully hidden beneath a large rock.

Suspended by ropes from the underside of the rock were 12 large parcels. After attaching her new capture to the rock, the spider ran out the door (one of them) of her nest and left the boy alone.

He was not really alone. The boy could see (sort of) through the walls of his shroud. It was like peering through a wall of milk. On both sides of him were more mummies. Beetles.

"How are you?" the boy asked one of the beetles.

The beetle made a noise, a grunt.

"Been here long?"

"Grunt."

Hours later, the spider returned. Hungry. She halted beside one of the beetles and tore open its shroud. Working her head into the opening she had made, she used her tusks to bite through the hard shell of the beetle inside and inject it with solvent. Inside its exoskeleton, the beetle slowly turned into jam. The spider pushed her head farther into the hole and sucked up the liquified beetle, every drop of him. When she was finished, she stripped the shroud off the empty carapace, wadded the silk into a ball, and swallowed it whole. She tossed what was left of the beetle onto a trash pile which consisted entirely of the remains of her other victims.

When she was finished, she crept up to the boy and inspected him with her row of eyes. "What type of food is it, hmm?"

"As I told you, I am poisonous," the boy said. "That is all you need to know!"

"It is food, but it stinks."

"Instant death!" the boy said. "Don't even think about it!"

"Are it a soft-body?" The spider backed away from the boy, rotating one way and then the other to show the boy to each of her six eyes.

The boy thought about telling the spider that obviously he was a soft-body, since he did not have an exoskeleton.

Having nothing better to do, the boy closed his eyes and fell asleep and dreamed that he was running in the sunlight, happy and safe.

When the boy awoke, he was still trapped. The spider was crouched in the middle of her nest. She was so motionless she might have been a hairy rock. Every few hours, almost imperceptibly, one of her eight legs twitched.

The boy tried many times to convince the spider that she should release him. He told her that he was so poisonous, just by remaining close to him, she might get sick and die.

"Even the fumes will probably kill you!" For safety's sake, she should push him out of her nest, tear open his shroud, and encourage him to run away.

He might as well have been shouting at the wind. The spider paid no attention to him.

Radiating in a hundred directions from her nest were nearly invisible ropes of silk. Whenever an insect stumbled over one of them, the spider burst out of her nest and nipped the fellow. The poison that dripped from her fangs did not kill her victims but paralyzed them. Then she turned her prey into another mummy and hung it inside her nest beside all the others.

While the boy hung there inside his shroud, trapped and helpless, she captured two flies, four more beetles, and a cricket.

"You have more food than you can possibly eat," the boy said. "Why capture more, greedy?"

The spider squatted in the middle of her nest.

"Are it coming?" she whispered. "Do it want its way?"

As the time passed, the boy began to feel sorry for himself. Day after day, hour after hour, hanging in a bag, starving to death–it gets a fellow down. By the fourth day, he could no longer tell the difference between his dreaming and waking life. Often, the boy imagined he saw his mother gazing at him, her eyes full of tears. Sometimes he thought he could hear his mother's voice calling his name.

The fifth day of the boy's imprisonment, a male spider poked his head into one of the entrances of the nest. Although she was twice the size of the male, the female spider did not kill him.

"You have a visitor," the boy said.

Very slowly, the male entered the nest. The female trained two of her eyes on him but did not move a single leg.

The male spider began to dance, high-stepping in place. Then he began to tiptoe all around the big female until the two spiders were face-to-face.

For half an hour, neither of them moved.

At last, the female permitted the small male to roll her over onto her back. The male roped each of her eight legs to the floor of the nest and then carefully climbed up onto her abdomen and began to do push-ups.

The whole business was over in a minute. The little male attempted to hop down from the huge female, but he seemed dazed and confused. He fell to the floor of the nest and turned in a circle as if he no longer remembered where he was. He almost seemed drunk.

While the male was bumping into bags of prey, the female began to return to life. One by one, her legs pulled free of the ropes the male had used to glue her to the floor of the nest. Flailing her legs, she flipped herself over until she was upright again.

"Run!" the boy yelled. "Run for your life, you stupid idiot!"

The male took a wobbly step toward the exit he had used to enter the nest, but he was too slow.

A minute later, the female hung a new bag to the roof of the nest.

Days passed. The boy lost all sense of time.

The female's abdomen began to swell until it grew so fat and heavy, it dragged on the ground.

One afternoon, the female spider began to vibrate and grunt. From her abdomen oozed a ball full of something that looked like honey. Another golden ball slid out of her. And another. They were not really balls of honey. They were not even eggs. They were tiny, newly born, almost transparent spiders. Each brand-new creature trembled and jerked and finally began to crawl toward its mother. The tiny spiders found places to perch on her back until she was almost completely covered with them.

The boy could hear the babies whispering.

"Food! More food! More food! We must have food! More!"

Every day, the female pulled herself to a bag and tore it open. The little spiders crowded down around her head and dropped into the sack. Each time, when the babies emerged from the bag, they were a little fatter, a little less transparent, a little stronger.

The female began to lose weight. The whispers of her children urged her on and on.

"More food! More!"

The largest of the babies ate the smaller babies. "Food! Must have more! More!" Their exoskeletons grew thicker and darker and finally sprouted hair.

After she opened the final bag, the one containing what was left of their father, the spider mother crept to the top of her nest. She let herself down on a rope and dangled there — another bag of food.

The baby spiders emerged from the bag that had contained their father. They looked like adult spiders now, brown and hairy.

"More food! More! More!"

The mother spider bit herself, injected herself with the dissolving poison, turned herself into a bag of stew — one last meal for her ever-hungry offspring.

Inside his bag, the boy wept — not for the mother spider. For himself. How long would he have to hang here in his bag? Forever? Why did no one come to save him? Would he die here, alone and forgotten?

After the spider children finished consuming their mother, they discovered there was one bag left in the nest.

"Food! More food! More!"

Crawling to the top of the nest, the little spiders lowered themselves onto the last bag of food. They tore it open.

No sooner did the spiders tear a large hole in the bag than they began to smell the poison.

"Nasty! What is it?! Stinky! Ick!" They retreated. "Not food! Not food! Danger!"

When the boy's arms were free, he finished tearing his bag apart. By the time he kicked loose from the bag and fell to the floor of the nest, the last spider was escaping out the door.

"Food! Food! More food!"

The boy crawled out of the nest on his hands and knees. He stood up in the sunlight and —

Here, Ronald stopped writing the story. What did his hero do next? He had no idea. He read over what he had written, making little changes. He wondered if it was in fact possible for a boy to live that many days without food or drink. 14 days? 21 days without any nourishment? It probably wasn't possible.

Ronald sighed and laid down on his bed. Story-writing was hard.

CHAPTER 6: WE ALSO LIKE LOVE STORIES

"It doesn't do any good to mope," Cook said. She was staring out Ronald's window.

Ronald said, "Go away! If I want to mope, I'm going to! Who are you waving at?"

Cook was staring out his window at something. "Those fools out there. Shoo! Go away! Scat!"

"Let me look!"

Two girls were standing in the yard just beyond Ronald's window. Neither of them was Mary Margaret. One girl was plump. She had brown hair (bangs) and brown eyes (behind glasses). The other girl was tall and skinny. She had blonde hair and blue eyes (no glasses). The girls appeared to be about the same age as Mary Margaret.

The girls were saying something, making gestures and attempting to communicate.

"Go see what they want!" Ronald said.

Cook said she had seen these girls before. "They live down the street. Go away! I'll call the police!"

Ronald soon found it embarrassing to be stared at by girls and moved away from the window. He was wearing his pajamas. He told Cook, "Go out there! Are they Girl Scouts?" Ronald had heard that Girl Scouts go door-to-door selling cookies. He was not allowed to eat cookies.

Cook grumbled, but she went to see what the girls wanted. That was no simple chore because, before she could return to Ronald, Cook had to take a disinfecting shower and change her clothes.

When Cook returned an hour later, she said, "It's just like I said. They live down the street. They said they are best friends with your girlfriend Mary Margaret. One of them lives behind her and the other one lives at the end of the block, in the pink house with the porch. One of them is named Jan and the other one is Ann, but don't ask me which is which because I already forgot."

"What do they want?"

"They want to know is it true what Mary Margaret told them, that you have a disease and if you set foot outdoors everyone in this neighborhood will die."

"That isn't true! That's crazy! Why would she say that? Did you tell them about my condition?"

"I told them."

Ronald looked out the window again, but the girls were gone. He wished Cook had kept her mouth shut about his condition because he rather liked the idea of being a dangerous boy with a contagious disease that could kill everyone. That seemed much better than being a boy who has to hide in his room all the time because the outside world with its pollen and germs wants to kill him.

"Do you think they'll come back?"

"They're coming back tomorrow. Oh, here's the funny part. You know that story you wrote, the one about the praying mantis? The one I took out to Mary Margaret?"

"What about it?"

"She told them about it. Told them it was too scary for normal girls like them. It would give them nightmares. She wouldn't let them read it. So now, guess what? They want to read it to prove they can't be scared."

"They *want* to read it?"

"I told them I'd deliver the message. If you're OK with it, I'll Scotch-tape your story to the front door. They can come get it."

Ronald wanted to yell at Cook for saying such a thing — without his permission! On the other hand, now that he knew the two girls existed, he wanted them to read his story.

Ronald got very little sleep that night because he kept thinking about the two girls and how they might react to his story. He had decided to give them his new story, the one about the spider-mother. He thought it was scarier than the one about the praying mantis.

The next day, the spider-mother story was Scotch-taped to Ronald's front door. On the envelope containing it, Ronald had written:

THIS STORY MAY CAUSE NIGHTMARES!

He asked Cook, "Do you think they will really, truly read it?" He had asked Cook that same question about a hundred times.

Ronald wished he had made a copy of his story about the spider-mother who sacrificed herself for her children. He tried to imagine Ann and Jan reading it. He remembered bits of it he liked and wondered if the girls would like those bits, or would they hate his story and hate him for writing it.

A day passed. The girls did not return. Two more days passed. Ronald concluded the girls had either forgotten to read his stupid story, or worse, they'd read it and hated it! They were just too polite to tell him.

On the fourth day, Cook found Ronald's story and its envelope in the mailbox. She microwaved the story and disinfected herself, and then carried the story into his room. It was in poor condition. The pages had been folded and refolded and someone had spilled something on it — chocolate milk? One page was torn and repaired with tape. The envelope also contained an extra page with two kinds of handwriting on it.

Dear Ronald, we are sorry your story got ripped but it's not our fault because my brother Max grabbed it.

Max is a thief and a jerk, just like my brother.

He thinks your story would be better if the boy would stomp some of the spiders and get spider guts all over his shoes. He is a stupid boy.

I like your story.

We both like horror stories. Even if they are about bugs. We don't really like bugs.

We did not get nightmares.

We were glad the boy escaped the nest in the end, but it would be better if the baby spiders eat him.

That would be a lot more scary.

Mary Margaret said you were going to put her in one of your stories, is that true, because she is not in the spider story. We are wondering if you could put us in a story?

We think a story with two girls in it would be very interesting.

Especially if the girls rescued the boy from something super scary like a giant scorpion. Scorpions are super-duper scary!

Thank you for letting us read your story. Good luck with everything.

Jan P and Ann W.

PS We like horror best but we also like love stories.

CHAPTER 7: THE DELICATE SCORPION

Ronald read the relevant chapter in Dr. Fabber's guidebook and found out it was unlikely a scorpion would be living in his back yard because scorpions usually reside in deserts. Some varieties have mating dances that involve dozens of scorpions at the same time. That sounded interesting. He also learned that, despite their weapons (claws and poison-tipped stingers), scorpions are not very brave. He got the impression that Dr. Fabber considered the average scorpion a coward.

It took Ronald a week to write the story. It had to be good, and it needed to contain a girl or two. This proved difficult. He tried to add two girls, a large one with brown hair and glasses and a tall one with blond hair and blue eyes, but the story seemed to have a mind of its own. It wanted to be about a scorpion, not two girls. Maybe if his story included a girl scorpion that would be almost as good.

He asked Cook, "When you were young, did you ever go to a dance?"

"You mean — like a prom? Of course. I was in the Queen's Court!"

Cook told him, on prom night, the girls got dressed up in gowns and high heels, and the boys bought them corsages, and then the boys drank beer and got into fights over the girls. The couples danced and held each other close. Cook described the mirror ball and explained how it threw spots of light in every direction, and how the gym was decorated with streamers and balloons.

"Why do you care about this stuff?"

"I'm working on a story about scorpions." Ronald explained that scorpions have this mating dance they do. And he asked Cook what a sperm packet is.

"A what?"

"The males deposit this thing called a sperm packet, and then they maneuver the female until they get her on top of it."

Cook told Ronald he was not allowed to give the neighbor girls a story about a sperm packet.

"Don't put anything like that in there."

"Why not?"

"Never you mind why not! Because I say so!"

A HORRIFYING LOVE STORY
by Ronald Matthews

Like horses, scorpions have eyes on the sides of their head and so they are unable to see what is directly in front of them. While the boy was standing on top of dry, sandy, desert soil wondering where he might get a drink of water, a scorpion lurched forward and bumped right into him.

"Hey!" the boy said. "Watch where you're going!"

When he saw the scorpion, the boy just about fainted. The arachnid was enormous. It had two huge black claws and a terrifying stinger.

The scorpion backed up as fast as he could. He ran into his burrow and blocked up its entrance with a pile of stones. "Go away!"

The boy laughed out loud because the scorpion was three times his size.

Inside his burrow, the scorpion burst into sobs.

"Please," the boy said, "for heaven's sake, don't carry on so. I didn't mean to frighten you." The idea that the terrifying scorpion was afraid of him was amazing to the boy.

"Ooh, ooh, ooh! Oh, go away! Go away!"

"Please, stop crying!"

"What's the use? Ooo, ooo, ooo!"

"Then don't stop! I mean if you LIKE crying, I'll leave you to it."

"Ooo, ooo, boo-hoo! What?"

"Goodbye! I'm leaving!"

The scorpion removed a stone from the entrance to his burrow and maneuvered his body so that one of his eyes could look out through the hole where the stone had been. "Don't go away. Please." The scorpion pushed down the wall of stones it had created and emerged from his burrow, dragging his tail and its lethal weapon behind him.

"What in the world is the matter with you?"

"I," the scorpion lifted one claw into the air and pressed it tragically to his brow, "am without — love!"

The boy had no idea how to respond to this confession. "Well, then, OK. But if it's just THAT ...? If it's just love ..."

"Just love?!" the scorpion thrust his claws high into the air. "Just heart! Just blood! Just life!"

The boy made sure there were several large rocks between himself and the scorpion.

"There must be plenty of female scorpions nearby. Don't you think at least one of them will find you attractive?"

The scorpion stiffened and his tail rose into the air. "Only one? Sir, did you say, did you DARE to say ONLY ONE?"

"Sorry! MANY of them. HUNDREDS of them will find you irresistible. Calm down!"

"I am said to be one of the most handsome and elegant scorpions of this age."

"OK."

"It is not a question of physical appeal."

"What then?"

"Delicacy, sir!"

The boy was unable to think of any reply.

"Sir, you see before you a scorpion with an exaggerated sensitivity to," the stinger waved in the air, "to coarseness!"

"I'm not sure what you —"

"To vulgarity, sir!"

"You've run into that sort of thing lately? Vulgarity and, uh, coarseness?"

"Does EVERY NIGHT seem 'lately' enough for you, sir?"

"Every?"

"NIGHTLY, I am forced to endure scenes of UNBELIEVABLE," the stinger began to whip through the air as the tail coiled and uncoiled, "RUDENESS, SIR!"

The boy retreated several more steps to make sure he was out of range.

"Where exactly do you encounter this, uh, rudeness, if you don't mind telling me?"

"When everything has turned blue! The Dance, sir!"

"I'm not sure I'm following. What dance?"

"THE DANCE!" The Scorpion raised his claws above his head and clicked them like castanets.

"My goodness," the boy said.

"Observe my footwork, sir!"

The boy retreated another step. "Very nice."

The scorpion, with his pincers held high, performed a figure 8. "I am one of the most thrilling dancers ever seen, sir!"

"I don't doubt it. But since you are so handsome and such an excellent dancer, what's the trouble? Why don't the females like you?"

"The trouble, sir, is the age! If one is refined, accomplished, talented, and one is STILL SCORNED, is it not obvious? We live in the Age of the Oaf!"

Guessing that the "oaf" might be another male scorpion, the boy suggested that maybe tonight the rival would not appear.

"If one oaf does not attend, another one will!" The scorpion retreated into his burrow. "The shadows are lengthening, sir! I must prepare!"

Shortly after sunset, when the sky had turned purple and pink, dozens of scorpions emerged from their burrows and made their way to a large flat area, their dancing floor. The boy hid and watched. It was terribly dangerous to be around so many scorpions, but all of them seemed preoccupied. They did not even notice him.

The boy soon realized it was easy to identify the female scorpions because they were much larger than the males. The scorpions lined up at each end of the dance floor, the males at one end and the females at the other. The females strutted back and forth. Occasionally, they paused to examine their claws. The males poked one another with their tails and made predictions as to what they would soon be doing to the females.

The Delicate Scorpion stood beside the boy, curling and uncurling his tail. "Dolts! Boobs! Oafs!"

"Why don't they start dancing?" the boy asked.

"Because the LAST thing any oaf is capable of is doing ANYTHING on his own." The other males were now pinching one another, laughing loudly, and pretending they did not notice the females.

The Delicate Scorpion crossed the dance floor and bowed to the largest of the females. She was almost twice his size. After capturing her pincers in his own, he led her onto the floor. As if a button had been pushed, the other males surged across the floor to the females. In a minute, the entire dance floor was occupied by pairs of dancing scorpions.

The Delicate Scorpion led the large female three times around the floor, but then another male ran up to him and his partner and dragged their pincers apart. The Delicate Scorpion held onto the female with one of his pincers and tried to push away the other male with the other. The other male grabbed the female's free pincer with his left claw and the

Delicate Scorpion's left with his right. Briefly, the three of them circled each other in a triangular dance. But at last, the interloper managed to pull the female loose and capture both her pincers in his own. The Delicate Scorpion was forced to retreat.

"There! You see what I endure, sir!" The scorpion stabbed the air with his stinger.

"But I don't understand. Why did you let him cut in?'

"She asked me to, sir!"

"Oh, dear."

"She prefers that oaf to, to ME!"

The scorpion stared at his rivals and muttered poisonous critiques of their dancing skills.

At last, he ran around the edge of the dance floor to where a very long female with exceptionally large claws had been left stranded by her last partner. A moment later, he pulled his capture out onto the floor, where he and she performed several intricate maneuvers, culminating in an astonishing double-headstand. While still holding hands, so to speak, the two scorpions pushed their tails straight up into the air and touched their stingers together.

This maneuver had so great an effect on the unoccupied males that they began to imitate the Delicate Scorpion by clutching one another and performing the double-headstand. They kept this up until they fell over, laughing. The mockery caused the female with the large claws to pull away from the Delicate Scorpion and run from the floor, holding her pincers over her face and sobbing.

A minute later, the scorpion was standing beside the boy again.

The boy thought it best to say nothing.

"Perhaps you are wondering why I allow myself to be humiliated this way night after night."

"Not at all."

"Sir, you see before you the dupe, the mark, the prey of love."

The boy said, "Well, er...."

"You see before you a worm, sir. A caterpillar."

"But why do you try? I mean, if it's as hopeless as you say."

"Are you aware what happens to a caterpillar who refuses to turn into a butterfly?"

The boy shook his head.

"He REMAINS a caterpillar! He remains a caterpillar for the REST OF HIS LIFE!"

The boy's forehead wrinkled as he thought about this comment. "It seems to me that, in a way, your accomplishments are against you."

"Exactly, sir. My point made perfectly."

"The oafs seem to do quite well with the ladies."

"Indeed, they do."

"This is just an idea. Maybe you could, well, in a way, BECOME an oaf."

"What?"

"Only a brilliant actor could pull it off, of course, but with all your talents and accomplishments, maybe..."

Ten minutes later, a swaggering oaf plowed through the dancers. After tripping several dancers and adding to the fun by tipping over an elderly female, the oaf cornered a large female and yelled, "Come on, babycakes, you wanna dance with a REAL scorpion?" The female was dancing with another male, a small one, who panicked, let go of his partner, and ran away as fast as his eight legs could carry him.

The oaf yelled, "Run, baby boy, come back when you grow up!" He grabbed one of the female's pincers. "What are we waiting for, baby?"

After dragging the large female around the floor three times, the oaf yelled, "Wanna get outta this mob, sweetie? Come on, we'll get a little fresh air." The oaf pulled the female away from the floor and toward his burrow.

"I love you, baby. No kidding. Wouldn't say so if it weren't true. You do something to me!" The oaf dragged the female across his doorstep. "Come in, baby. Don't be like that. I really need it. You don't know how it is for a guy. Just let me rub your tail."

The female resisted, giggling, but despite her resistance, she was at last pulled entirely into the oaf's burrow.

"Come on, baby. Just let me. Trust me. You know I love you. Oh, God! Oh, don't stop! Oh, baby, you're killing me! Oh! Oh!"

The next morning, when the boy peeked into the scorpion's burrow to say goodbye, he discovered the burrow contained no one except the female, who was finishing her breakfast.

"Hello," the boy said. "Is the man of the house in?"

"The what?

"The male scorpion who lives here. Has he gone out?"

"Oh, him. He isn't out, honey. He's in!"

"Excuse me?"

"In me, sweetie."

"In you? How could he...?"

"I just ate him, dearie."

"You ate him?!"

"What else would I do with him?"

"But that's horrible!"

"He was a bit dry." The female picked her teeth with a long slim object that the boy recognized as his friend's stinger.

"I don't mean HE was horrible," the boy yelled. "I mean YOU are! You're nothing but a horrid cannibal!"

"What a silly idea. Of course, I'm not horrid. My friends say I'm very sweet. Besides, all the girls eat them. We're so hungry afterward. And they just lie there." She picked her teeth.

"It's perfectly sensible to eat them. Now, go away. It's time for my sunbath."

CHAPTER 8: THE MOTH

Ronald was in a bad mood because he had discovered the girls Ann and Jan had never gotten a chance to read his story about the Delicate Scorpion. He had instructed Cook to Scotch-tape the story to the front door so the girls could read it. Had she done that? No! Instead, Cook had read his story and returned it to him, telling him no way was she going to give that story to the girls.

"Why not?"

Cook pressed her lips together.

"It's too suggestive."

"Suggestive! What does that even mean?"

"Never you mind."

"But it does not say one word about sperm packets!"

"You can write them a different story. A better story! Your hero should get caught by the scorpion and then them two girls can come and rescue him. What could be simpler? Nothing about dancing! Nothing about mating! And for the love of God, no more cannibalism!"

"Is it my fault that all insects ever care about is eating and mating?"

Cook was adamant. She would not give his story to the girls.

Ronald was furious. He hated Cook. He thought about telling her that, in his experience, it did no good to try to force a story to be this way or that way. The story would come out the way it wanted. All you had to do was get out of its way. He thought Cook would probably never understand. She was too stupid. It was a waste of time to try to teach her anything.

Cook said, "Why can't you write a nice story about a beautiful butterfly? Or even better, rabbits? I bet them girls would love a story about nice bunny rabbits. No one needs a story about insects that are cannibals!"

"But they like horror. They said they did. Horror stories and love stories. That's what I wrote. A horrible love story!"

"I hate talking to you when you're like this, Mister Grumpy-Pants! You are right and everyone else is wrong. I have things to do! I'll come back when you calm down!"

Cook left the room. The door automatically sealed behind her, and the air purifier turned on.

Ronald thought, *She's the one who should calm down!* He vowed he would never again write a story. What was the point? The world did not deserve any more of his stories. Unfortunately, it was fun to write them; it was like falling into a dream. After an hour or so, he found himself opening the *Guide* and looking at the pictures of butterflies and moths.

He discovered that butterflies and moths have no sense of hearing. Hardly any insects can hear, only the noisy ones like cicadas and crickets. He found out that butterflies and moths have few natural enemies except birds. They have very long tongues so they can lick up the nectar at the bottom of flowers. They aren't really tongues. Butterflies have a proboscis, a long tube which many people think of as a tongue. It's like their mouths turn into straws. Butterflies and moths are not the same thing. Butterflies have colorful wings and shiny black bodies. They fold their wings vertically over their backs and prefer the daylight. Moths like darkness. Usually, they are smaller than butterflies and have drab wings and hairy bodies. They fold their wings in a way that conceals their abdomens. There are exceptions. Some moths have large, beautiful wings, for example Luna Moths.

It occurred to Ronald that his characters could be in hell. That would explain the fact they could hear and talk. He kind of liked the idea. Hell seemed an excellent location for horror stories. Unfortunately, he did not know much about hell. His mother did not believe in it. Besides, why would his hero the boy be stuck in hell? The boy didn't seem especially bad. Ronald wondered what horrible sin the boy could have committed that he would wind up in hell. So far, the boy hadn't done anything the least bit bad except insult the wizard; he'd compared the wizard's nose to a potato. That hardly seemed a serious sin. And don't you have to die before you can go to hell? If he said all the characters are in hell, he would then have to explain what horrible thing every single character did when still alive. Then he would have to explain how each one died. He felt himself getting a stomachache and lay back on his bed.

Ronald's ceiling was painted blue and covered in plastic stars. At night when the lights were switched off, the stars glowed.

Maybe he should write a story about the evil wizard who shrank the boy in the first place. Probably the boy's mom went crazy with grief after her only son disappeared. He could write about that. Maybe the wizard took advantage of the boy's mom and convinced her to marry him. Probably they were on their honeymoon in some place like India. Obviously, the boy should quit messing around with insects and grow big again so he could rescue his mother from the evil wizard.

Ronald sighed. Stories were too difficult, especially if everything had to connect and make sense.

What about the red-headed girl who rode on the back of a grasshopper and was looking for her father, Dr. Fabber, the author of *The Intelligent Boy's Guide to Insects and Spiders*? Maybe the evil wizard lost something very valuable, but it was also very small. And the girl had to find it, or else she would never be allowed to be big again. What would the little valuable thing be? Oh, this was all getting much too complicated!

Ronald closed his eyes and decided he would take a nap. When he woke up, he would follow Cook's advice and write a nice story about a bunny rabbit, a story that would not contain anything "suggestive."

When Ronald awoke, he did write a story. Unfortunately, it did not contain a bunny rabbit.

THE LUNA
a story by Ronald Matthews

One night, unable to sleep, the boy crawled out from beneath a dead leaf and looked up at the sky. Despite the darkness, he could see many things. A thousand stars were visible, shining down steadily. A huge full moon hung just above the horizon. The boy knew that the grass jungle contained many dangerous predators, spiders and centipedes, assassin beetles. He shivered and crouched down. And yet, as he hugged his knees and looked up at the sky full of stars, the world seemed peaceful and quiet and safe.

Above him, the boy saw something floating in the sky, a pair of green sails. For a moment he wondered if it was a kind of airship, tacking one way and then another in the breeze. He realized what it was. Not a ship. A Luna moth. Its wings were huge and beautiful. In the soft moonlight, the wings were a pale dreamy green, like sails made of green ice. The Luna landed on top of a night-blooming flower. The huge wings closed around the body of the moth as it dipped its head into the mouth of the flower and used its long black proboscis to drink the flower's nectar.

Unable to keep quiet, the boy cried, "You're so beautiful! Oh!" The Boy said "oh" because, when the moth lifted its head from the flower, parted its wings, and examined him with its faceted eyes, it revealed its fat, hairy body.

"Go away," said the Luna. The boy tiptoed closer. The wings seemed to glow as if they were phosphorescent, as if elves had touched them up with magic paint.

"Did you fail to hear what I just said? Go away!"

The boy froze when he was still a safe distance from the Luna. Although he was pretty sure the moth would not harm him, it pays to be cautious. The vast wings parted again and then closed like a tent over the moth's abdomen. The wings were unbelievably beautiful, but the moth's body was dark and hairy.

"No doubt, you find me irresistible." The Luna sighed as if to be so beautiful was a burden. "If you cannot take your eyes off of me, at least say something amusing."

The boy wondered what he could possibly say that would amuse a moth.

"If you cannot speak, perhaps you can dance." The great wings opened and closed and opened again. The boy had a sudden memory of his mother and how, when he was small, she liked to play peek-a-boo with him, covering her pretty eyes with her pretty hands and then letting him see her beautiful face. Except in this case, the effect was the opposite. When the gorgeous green wings parted, what was revealed was not the least bit beautiful.

"Dance?" the boy said. "I don't know how."

"Can't dance. Can't talk. What are you good for? Anything? Can you sing?"

"Not very well," the boy said. He took a step closer to the moth. "I'm sorry, but your wings! They are so beautiful!"

The Luna spread her wings, displaying them in all their glory. They seemed impossibly lovely, as if they were made of ghosts, the ghosts of beautiful people. They were elegant and perfect. No bird had yet managed to take a bite out of either of them.

"Do not bother trying to think of pretty compliments. Compliments bore me." The Luna opened and closed her wings, revealing and concealing her hairy body. The boy took another step closer to her, hypnotized by the contrast of the superb wings and the insect's ugly body.

"I see you are still human." The moth inspected the boy with her compound eyes. "Nearly."

The boy was startled and did not know how to reply. What could she mean? He was NEARLY human?

"I too was human. Once upon a time. Thank goodness, all THAT is over."

"You were ... human?" The boy felt as if he was waking up from a dream, as if someone had pinched him awake. "That is not even possible!"

"You will discover that everyone here was once human." The Luna looked at the boy again, spreading her wings.

The boy retreated a step and then two more steps.

"Everyone? You're lying. You're nothing but a big fat liar!"

"We all start out like you — soft. Stupid. No doubt, you are a newcomer."

The boy thought about telling her the story, how the only reason he was stuck here in the grass forest was because an evil wizard shrank him, but decided it was none of her business. What did she mean, he was ALMOST human?

The moth said, "I am practically a newcomer myself."

"If you do not mind me asking," the boy said, "how long have you been here?"

"A short time." The Luna arranged her wings so they would catch the next puff of breeze. "Three hundred years."

"Three — hundred — years!"

"You must be delighted you escaped."

"What do you mean? Escaped from what?"

"From the other world, the dreary one. I hardly think of it anymore. Well, do not worry. I'm sure your transformation will soon begin." She looked down at the boy. "I suppose you will turn into something nasty. Most men do."

Now that the boy could see the Luna plainly, he concluded that, except for her lovely wings, she was one of the most hideous creatures he had ever met. Obviously, she was completely insane.

"Goodbye, foolish boy." The Luna spread her wings and floated into the air. She rose higher and higher and again reminded the boy of a sailing ship. Never in his life had he seen a more beautiful sight than that of the Luna moth floating in the night air, and yet all he could think of was her thick and hairy body, now invisible in the moonlight.

CHAPTER 9: ANOTHER STORY ABOUT A BEETLE

Saturday, Ronald received another postcard from his mother. This one was a picture of a Hindu woman with a red spot on her forehead and a golden ring in her nose. His mother's elegant handwriting was on the back.

"We're having so much fun! We're going to extend our honeymoon another month, flying to our favorite place in the whole wide world, Paris. Are we crazy, or what? All our Love, Mom."

Ronald sighed and put the postcard on top of his little stack of similar postcards.

Cook sat down in the armchair and said, "Oh, don't be a Gloomy Gus. I'm ready to read your new story. This one better be decent." She put on her reading glasses, and Ronald handed her his story about the Luna moth.

While Cook was reading the story, two boys wearing baseball caps appeared outside Ronald's window. One boy was large and the other was skinny and blond. Ronald had an impulse to hide from the boys but then he just stood there in the window wearing his pajamas and let them look at him. He waved his hand at the boys. He made himself smile.

"Hi," he said, though he knew they couldn't hear him.

One of the boys, the large one, had brought a notebook of ruled paper and a marker pen. He wrote something on a page of the notebook and held it up: MAX. The large boy pointed at himself. Then he handed the notebook to the blond boy.

That boy wrote JOSH on a page and held it up, pointing to himself with his free hand.

Ronald pointed at himself and said, "Ronald!"

Max grabbed the notebook and wrote: *CAN YOU COME OUT?*

Ronald shook his head no.

Max wrote: *ARE YOU SICK?*

Ronald nodded his head.

Josh grabbed the notebook away from Max and wrote: *CAN WE HAVE A STORY?*

Cook said, "It's possible them boys will like this story, but I doubt it. In my experience, what boys like is a story with plenty of fighting in it. This story doesn't have any fighting and besides, it's yucky."

Ronald folded up the moth story and stuffed it into an envelope. On the outside of the envelope, he wrote PLEASE RETURN. When Cook was not looking, he also folded up the scorpion story and pushed it into the envelope.

By the time Ronald gave the envelope to Cook, the boys were out in the field playing catch and were soon joined by more boys. They organized into teams and started a baseball game. Cook had explained the rules of baseball to Ronald: four bases, balls, and bats. Gloves. Three strikes and you're out. Single, double, triple. Homerun!

When Cook returned, she assured him the envelope was Scotch-taped to the front door, but she doubted the boys would even remember to look for it. "Here's an idea, honey. Maybe you should write them a story about baseball."

"Don't be stupid! Insects don't play baseball!"

He told Cook to buy him clothes like Josh and Max wore -- blue jeans, tee shirts, and baseball caps turned backwards.

"If it's OK with your mom," Cook said. "She pays the bills."

When Ronald woke from his nap and looked out of the window, the boys were gone. The field seemed empty without a pack of boys filling it with life, but in fact if you got down on your knees and peered into the grass you would find a million insects, ants, crickets, all sort of creatures.

"The envelope?" Ronald said.

"They come and got it," Cook said. "It's time to take your medicine."

That night, Ronald dreamed he was wearing his new clothes, jeans and a tee-shirt and a baseball cap turned backwards. He had a big leather glove on his hand and was playing baseball. Right field. The pitcher threw the ball, a fast ball right down the middle of the plate. The bat cracked and the ball sailed up and up and then started its downward path. Ronald was terrified he would mess up the catch and the other team would get a homerun. He lost the ball in the glare of the sun, but he stuck up his glove anyway. A miracle happened. The ball fell right into the glove. Yay, inning over! His team ran toward home plate. The other boys ran past him and banged him on the shoulder and yelled, "Nice catch!"

Three days later, the envelope returned. The boys had messy angular handwriting and had misspelled a few words.

"We like the scorpion specially the part when the girl scorpion eats him, thats pritty funny. We also like yer moth story. Its reel cool how the boy will turn into an ugly old bug especially if it can be the kind that eats other bugs. Make him a badass. A wasp. Or a big hairy tarantula. Best idea, he should have the power to turn into ANY insect! Insect Boy!"

A day later, a second note arrived in the mailbox, written by the girls.

"Our stupid brothers did not let us read the new stories. Is it true the boy in the story is going to turn into a tarantula? We don't like that idea. We hate spiders!! Your stories would be better if they include girls. At least one. And you should change the part about how the boy stinks. No one likes a stinky boy."

Ronald's paper basket filled up with failed stories. He tried to write about a baseball team called the Chicago Bugs, but he couldn't make it work. A story called The Chicago Centipedes did not work either. He tried to give his hero the superpower to turn into any insect including a tarantula, but how would the boy acquire such a power? He attempted a story about how the boy no longer smelled of poison. But how could he change that detail? If the boy was not poisonous, he would soon get eaten!

Ronald wished he had never planted the idea that the boy was going to transform into an insect, but that idea had just popped out of him. Sometimes an entire story just poured out of him without any trouble and seemed right. It was as if his hand wrote the story by itself. When that happened, it was almost a sin to change it.

It took a week, but Ronald finally finished another story. Unfortunately, it was not about baseball-playing insects, or a boy who turned into a tarantula, and it did not contain any girls.

THE BORING BEETLE
by Ronald Matthews

Nothing much happened that week except the boy was almost crushed by a cricket. When they decide to change their location, crickets (like fleas) leap high into the air and crash to earth wherever.

The boy slept in holes created by the kind of insects who leave behind a mess of heads and legs. There was almost nothing to eat except seeds and flowers. The boy developed a taste for violets, but he hated dandelions. Dandelions are nasty!

When the boy met the beetle, he was in a bad mood. The beetle immediately began telling him the story of her life. She had spent almost all of it boring a tunnel in a tree. The boy climbed up on top of her back and listened. Sort of. It is hard to remain interested in a boring beetle's life story because it is so, well, boring.

"And then, let me see, oh yes, I encountered a patch of oily wood that tasted like that other patch of oily wood, that patch I found just before I found that dry bitter patch."

Directly in the path of the beetle, a second beetle appeared. A male. The boy, because he was not totally stupid, jumped down and got out of the way. The female beetle continued to talk. She had many opinions about sap.

The male beetle was a big guy with a black horn growing out of his forehead. He waited for the female to crawl past him and then turned himself around and approached her from the rear. Without bothering to ask permission, he mounted her. Gripping her wing cases with his hind-legs, he raised up his head and midsection, and then thumped down against her. He did this several more times. Smack! Smack! Smack! The male rested for a moment while the female continued to lecture him about sap. To shut her up, the male whacked her on the head with one of his antennae.

Smack! Smack! Smack!

When he was finished, the male seemed too exhausted to move. He continued to sprawl on top of the female and made a clicking sound as if he contained a clock. With his front pair of legs, he grabbed the female's antennae and pulled back on them as if attempting to make her stop.

The female did not stop. She seemed to have forgotten she was carting a large male beetle on her back. She said, "I disliked that wood very much. It went on and on as if it would never end. Sometimes I felt close to despair. If this is the sort of wood a decent beetle must eat, tasteless and dry, day after day, hour after hour, well, what is the point? At long last — imagine my delight, I came to the end of that patch and discovered a vein of the most delicious wood I have ever eaten. Oh, it was tasty!"

Hours passed. The male seemed permanently glued to the female. Maybe he was dead.

The next day, the boy came across the female one more time. The male was no longer on top of her. Probably he had fallen off. She was crawling slowly toward a tree, talking, lecturing the air about the time she transformed from a larva into an adult.

"How eerie, how strange, and yet in a way, only what I expected."

The beetle started to crawl up the side of the tree. The boy decided to catch a ride. He caught hold of the edge of her wing cases and let her carry him up the side of the tree. If she carried him high enough, he would gain a panoramic view of the entire grass forest. Maybe he would locate the girl he had briefly met, the red-haired girl who had been riding on the back of a grasshopper. He would love to see her again; the boy was getting a little sick of never meeting anyone except insects, especially since half the insects he met wanted to eat him and would have devoured him, except for the fact he stunk of poison.

The female beetle did not seem to care that she was carrying a smelly boy on her back. The bark of the tree was so full of cracks and warts she had no trouble ascending. She climbed higher and higher until she was so high, the boy got nervous and tried not to look down.

At last, the beetle arrived at her hole, the mouth of the tunnel she had created when still a larva. She spent a few moments exploring the opening with her antennae and then tipped herself into it.

The boy jumped off her back and looked around. The beetle disappeared into the gloom of the tunnel. The boy followed her. Soon, they were in complete darkness. The boy hesitated.

Beetles do not mind darkness because they have an excellent sense of smell. The boy had a nose, but his sense of smell was not that great. What might the darkness ahead of him contain?

The boy groped his way forward, following the beetle, until he encountered a door — a plug— made of compressed wood dust. The beetle had pushed past it, so the boy did the same.

Ahead of him, he could hear the beetle.

"Oh, dear," she said.

The boy realized he was in a chamber, much wider than the tunnel.

"Oh, dear. Oh, dear. Oh, dear." The boy heard a plop. And then another. Was the beetle relieving herself?

"Oh, dear." Plop.

Plop. Plop. Plop. Plop.

After an hour, the plopping noise ceased. The boy could hear the beetle making new noises, possibly heaping wood dust over whatever she had just excreted. When she finished, the beetle reversed herself and dragged herself forward until she bumped into the boy.

"Hey! Watch out!" the boy yelled.

The beetle grabbed hold of the boy with her forelegs and propelled him out of her chamber and back into the tunnel. She pushed the boy past the plug and down the tunnel, and probably would have tossed him out the front door, but then seemed to remember she had one more task. She dragged herself back to the plug and heaped up wood dust until she had completely blocked the opening to her chamber.

When finished, the beetle pulled herself toward the light at the end of her tunnel. The boy got out of her way. She no longer seemed to notice him. Eventually, the beetle emerged from her tunnel, opened her wing cases, spread her wings, and flew away. The boy sort of wished he had hitched a ride. Very likely she did not live much longer.

The boy broke through the plug of wood dust the beetle had made and returned to the chamber. He crawled around in the darkness until he found them, 56 eggs, each one about the size of a baseball.

The boy ate two eggs. Not too bad. They tasted like chicken soup. He was safe. He had plenty to eat. If he stood in the mouth of the tunnel and looked out, he could see almost the entire grass forest. But how in the world was he going to get down from the tree?

CHAPTER 10: BLOOD AND GORE

Cook taped Ronald's story about the Boring Beetle to the front door. The next morning, she reported that the story had disappeared. Ronald waited for a response from his readers, but five days came and went, and no one returned his story. No one visited the field either. On the sixth day, Ronald plunged into despair. Obviously, his stories were horrible and stupid. What was he thinking? Other kids would never like him now. Maybe his story got lost, dropped in a puddle or something, and they didn't want to tell him about it. It was so stupid to write a story about a boring beetle. What was he thinking? He should have written a story full of blood and gore, something exciting that Max and Josh would like.

That night, Ronald had a dream in which he turned into a boring beetle. In the dream, he developed a splitting headache, looked in a mirror, and — oh my goodness! — antennae had sprouted from his forehead. The message of the dream was obvious. *Ronald Matthews is boring.* No wonder the neighbor kids hated his stories. He had made a terrible mistake in his last story.

Vowing to do better, Ronald started working on a new story.

THE BAT, A BLOOD-CURDLING STORY THAT IS
NOT BORING,
by Ronald Matthews

Since he had no safe way to get down from the tree, the boy explored the tunnel the boring beetle had made on the other side of her egg chamber. Not only did he have to explore in complete darkness; he had to crawl around heaps of wood dust. After a while, he realized what wood dust is. It is the wood that travels through the interior of a boring worm and, after processing, oozes out the other end of the worm.

Yuck!

Soon, the boy discovered a second tunnel, made by a second worm. Then he discovered a third tunnel. He soon realized something scary. If he discovered and crawled down a few more of these branching tunnels, he might spend the rest of his life crawling around the interior of the tree, lost in the dark. The boy made several more explorations until he felt secure. At least there were plenty of eggs to eat.

One day, he discovered a tunnel that contained an actual boring worm, the larval form of the beetle. A boring worm's head is slightly smaller than the tunnel it creates. Its head contains a pair of enormous saw-toothed jaws surrounded by a set of organs shaped like picks and shovels. With this equipment, the worm chews its way through the inside of a tree, leaving behind it a tunnel and piles of wood dust. Its segmented body, thickly coated with dust, trails behind the enormous head.

This particular worm was so fat the boy could stand up in its tunnel without bumping his head. Putting out his hand, the boy tapped the flank of the worm.

"Hello?"

The worm stopped gnawing.

"What is it?"

"Don't bother to turn around," the boy said. "It's just me."

"I will turn, or not turn, exactly as I please."

"I only meant you don't need to on my account."

"You," the worm said, "do not exist."

Since they have spent their entire lives boring through trees, in utter darkness, boring worms believe themselves alone in the world.

The boy said, "Of course I exist. Don't be silly. If I don't, who are you talking to?"

"I am talking to myself," the worm said. It resumed its gnawing, making so much noise the boy could hardly hear himself think.

The boy kicked the worm.

"There, you stupid idiot!"

"Oof!" The worm quit chewing.

"I suppose you did THAT to yourself?"

"I will or will not do whatever I please."

The boy kicked him again, harder.

"Ouch!"

"You aren't talking to yourself. You're talking to me!"

"If it is not I, then it must be a type of food. There are ninety-nine known categories of good food and an equal number of categories of bad food. It is no doubt the hundredth category of bad food that kicks me."

"Don't be stupid!"

"The universe," the worm said, "consists of food I have not eaten, which lies ahead, and food I have already eaten, which lies behind. As this one hundredth category of bad food lies behind, then it is certain I have already eaten it, and it has passed through me and come out my other end."

"Stupid! Stupid!" the boy yelled. He kicked the worm one more time, turned on his heel, and went back the way he had come. Before he had gone too far, the boy turned back and again yelled, "Stupid!"

A few days later, at the end of a long tunnel, the boy discovered a boring pupa. After a worm munches its way to the outer edge of its tree, it gnaws a large chamber. It softens the walls of the chamber by chewing on them. Then the worm continues its tunnel until it almost eats through the tree's layer of bark. It stops when only a thin shell of bark remains. It returns to its chamber and blocks the entrance with a round plug that it manufactures from regurgitated wood pulp. It crawls into the middle of the chamber, collapses, and begins its transformation. Days later, its skin splits apart and reveals a soft white pupa, barely able to move. The pupa sleeps in its cushioned chamber. Inside its skin, it transforms slowly into an adult beetle. The beetle looks nothing like the pupa or the worm. The skin of the pupa splits and out crawls the beetle. If it is a male, it has a big horn in the middle of its forehead.

When the boy entered the chamber, the boring pupa had just begun to twitch. He touched it with his hand. He could feel the adult inside, squirming back and forth. With a loud ripping sound, the skin split. A male beetle crawled out. The beetle pushed the skin of his pupa away with his soft legs and then rested, drying in the cool air of the chamber.

When he was strong enough to walk, he waddled over to the plug and began gnawing on it.

The boy had an idea.

With a great heave, the beetle rolled the plug to one side and pulled himself through the opening.

The boy followed the path the beetle had made. The beetle was ripping apart the thin shell of bark that was all that separated it from the great world outside.

"Hello!" the boy said, as soon as a raggedy quadrangle of the outer world had become visible. It was nighttime, and a half moon filled the sky with milky light.

"What the …?" The beetle stared at the boy through its large complex eyes. "That you, baby?"

The boy took a giant step backwards.

"I am NOT your baby! Don't be silly! Don't worry, I am harmless."

The beetle peered at the boy.

"You seen any females around here?"

"Not up here, but I'm sure there are plenty out there." The boy gestured at the great outdoors.

The beetle resumed the destruction of the door. When he had finished, he turned around to look at the boy again.

"I have an idea," the boy said. "A favor to request. Hope you don't mind."

"There's plenty of them out there, hey?" the beetle said.

"Millions. I would like to hitch a ride."

"Oh, boy!" The beetle began to click rapidly. "See my horn?" The beetle turned to the side so the boy could see the horn growing out of his forehead. "You think I've got a big one?"

"Enormous."

"Think so?"

"Sure."

"I figured it was pretty big. Here, I'll get it in the light more, so you can see it better." The beetle dragged himself farther into the doorway until his horn was easy to see in the moonlight.

"It's huge."

"Oh, boy! Oh, boy!" Dragging itself through the doorway, the beetle cracked open his wing cases for the first time. "Ladies, here I come!"

The boy leapt onto the back of the beetle just as the insect launched itself from the tree. The boy had pictured a spiraling glide downward, the night breeze blowing through his hair, the dark world spinning slowly beneath them, and then an abrupt but safe landing. Unfortunately, the boy had neglected to take into account the laws of aerodynamics. Instead of sailing smoothly through the air, the suddenly top-heavy beetle tumbled out of control the moment the boy's weight was added to his.

The beetle and the boy cartwheeled toward the ground. If the boy had not been so terrified, he would have screamed. They were going to crash!

Probably there are many sensations which it is possible to recognize on the basis of faint clues, but the sensation of being swallowed alive by a bat is not one of them.

Before the beetle and the boy could reach the ground, the bat's wing struck them in midair, scooped them up, and tossed them into the bat's mouth. From the moment they hit the wing, the boy had no idea what was happening. Inside the bat's mouth, he couldn't see a darn thing. The bat's tongue, slimy and wet, hustled the beetle and the boy into — what? A cave? The cave began to swallow them. Its slimy walls grabbed the boy and, with a series of ripples, pulled him down a slippery narrowing tunnel, through a pair of doors that dilated just enough to admit him, and at last dropped him into a black pit, where he landed on a heap of beetles, mosquitoes, moths, and fireflies.

These creatures were in a state of shock. Many were partially crushed. Some were already dissolving in puddles of digestive fluids. The stench was stomach-churning, overwhelming, not to mention the noise. The entire ghastly, hellish scene was revealed intermittently by the flashing fireflies.

Although the boy did not fully understand what had just happened, he grasped the overall situation. He was in the belly of some vast beast. If he did not act quickly, he would either drown in digestive fluids or suffocate in stench. He waded through the pile of moaning insects until he arrived at the stomach wall. He located something useful, the saw-toothed mandible of — what? Maybe a scimitar beetle. With the sharp point of the mandible, the boy stabbed the softest spot he could find and began pushing the mandible into the stomach wall.

The boy had failed to consider the effect he might have upon the stomach's owner. Experiencing a sharp pain in its stomach, followed by an excruciating tearing, the bat lost control of itself. The boy and the other passengers inside the bat tumbled every which way. The boy held onto the mandible for dear life. The moment the boy regained his footing, he resumed sawing. The bat flipped in midair, swerved, screamed, and crashed. The collision with the ground broke its neck.

Once his senses returned, the boy resumed surgery. Blood squirted out in streams. The boy continued to saw until he opened a large vent in the side of the stomach wall. Hip-deep in blood, he pushed out of the stomach.

Once he was clear of the stomach, the boy had nothing between himself and freedom but a thick layer of fat, the inner and outer skin of the bat's belly, and a forest of thick, coarse hair. It took him hours to hack his way through all these layers, but at last the boy emerged from a hole in the side of the bat and fell onto the ground.

Crawling away from the bat, the boy vomited up everything he had eaten in the last 24 hours. The sun was rising.

It is horrible to be swallowed alive! Horrible! But wonderful to escape.

Wonderful!

The boy was so tired, so exhausted, he pulled a leaf over himself and fell straight to sleep.

CHAPTER 11: THIS STORY MAY MAKE YOU SICK

Ronald woke up at 3 AM. He used his bathroom and drank a glass of decontaminated water. He lay back on his bed and looked up at the stars on his ceiling until he fell asleep again.

The next morning, Ronald started a new story.

HAVE YOU SEEN THIS BOY?
A story by Ronald Matthews

After the boy disappeared, his mom was full of grief. Every night she was on her knees praying for his safe return. She placed photos of him all over her house and taped flyers to all the telephone poles for a mile in every direction. HAVE YOU SEEN THIS BOY? The evil wizard kept asking her to marry him. He offered to take her to Paris on a honeymoon, but she said she could never get married again, not until she held her missing son in her arms. The evil wizard didn't want to bring back the boy because, if the boy got normal size again, he would tell everyone the wizard was evil and used black magic to turn people into insects. Maybe you wonder why the wizard did bad creepy stuff like that? The wizard had a temper and couldn't bear being insulted or contradicted or interrupted. Like, if you said his nose looked like a potato, he got mad and shrank you. The wizard had shrunk so many people, he lived in constant fear insects would invade his house. The reason the wizard feared an invasion was because when he shrank people he didn't like, eventually they turned into insects. What if they wanted revenge? So, to keep himself safe, the wizard used lots of pesticides. The way some people use deodorant, that's how he used pesticides. He kept a squirt bottle of bug spray with him and squirted himself with it six times a day.

Cook brought Ronald his breakfast tray. While he was eating his cereal, she read his new story.

"Are you gonna finish this one?" she said.

Ronald said, "Why should I?"

"Someone's feeling ouchy today." Cook removed her reading glasses and put them in a pocket of her smock. "By the way, I forgot to tell you. You got another postcard."

"Is Mom coming home? Let me see it!"

The postcard was a picture of the giant HOLLYWOOD sign in Los Angeles. On the back of it, Ronald's mother had written:

Darling, can you believe it? We're in Hollywood! Having the time of our lives! Love, love, love you! XXXOOO

Two days later, while Ronald was lying on his bed, staring at the stars on his ceiling and feeling sorry for himself, the neighbor kids returned from their vacation. It turned out the three families had gone on a camping trip to a national park. They returned with sunburns and mosquito bites. Someone — Cook said she didn't know who — brought back Ronald's stories and left them in the mailbox. The envelope also included a brief note:

Did you miss us? We went camping. Mary Margaret got sunburn. Jan got poison ivy. I got stung by a wasp. I hate wasps! ANN.

Ronald read the message seven times. Maybe his readers did not hate his stories after all.

The next day he got another note, a longer one that may have been written in a hurry because it contained no punctuation:

Dear Ronald I loved your story about the beetle my friend Jan and I took turns reading it in the car Jan made a joke she said boring beetles are boring ha ha but she really liked it our stupid brothers did not like it I'm sorry but that's what they said they were hoping the boy would turn into an insect like the Luna moth said instead of just hanging out with a boring beetle when the hero does transform into a bug I want him to turn into a butterfly Jan wants him to turn into a hornet and sting someone hopefully her brother and that's why Max said he wants the boy to turn into an ugly spider and scare Jan because Jan hates spiders and I do too Josh wants him to turn into a tsetse fly and bite someone probably me because if a tsetse fly bites you then you get sleeping sickness and never wake up I think that idea is stupid so don't do it Your friend Ann

After Cook read the note from the neighbor girl, she said, "Why don't you write them kids a story about space pirates? The space pirates could kidnap a dinosaur or something. That could be fun."

It made Ronald anxious that his readers loved his idea that the boy was going to turn into an insect. He was going to have to decide what kind of insect his hero could turn into, maybe one of the social insects like an ant or a bee. The good thing about bees compared to ants is that bees can fly. Also, they have stingers. The unfortunate thing is if a bee uses its stinger ... well, it isn't good. The bee dies.

Ronald asked Cook to please tape his new story, the one about the Giant Bat, to the front door.

Cook insisted on reading it first.

Ronald watched her read. She was wearing a mask, so he couldn't see her expressions. He reminded Cook his readers loved horror. Cook continued to read. As she read, a wrinkle appeared above the mask between her eyes.

Ronald sighed. The wrinkle was a bad sign.

When she finished reading the story, Cook laid it in her lap.

"Did you hate it?" Ronald asked.

Cook said the two girls had come by that morning and asked if the sick boy wrote any more stories.

"What if I make it a little less bloody?" Ronald said.

Cook said, "I'm going to let them read your stories. All of them. Even this one. But you must promise not to get overly excited. And if even ONE of their parents complains, that's the end of it!"

"Thank you, thank you, thank you!" Ronald wanted to throw his arms around Cook and hug her, but he was not allowed to touch people, so he restrained himself.

Cook put the story about the bat in an envelope and taped it to the front door. On the envelope she wrote WARNING: THIS STORY MAY MAKE YOU SICK.

Four days later, Ronald got his reviews. The neighbor kids loved his bat story. Even the boys loved it. They said it was sickening in a good way. They passed it around the neighborhood and two more kids read it, and everyone said it was the best one yet, especially the part at the end when the boy cuts his way out of the bat.

Ann's brother Max wrote Ronald a note:

"What if the boy wakes up covered in blood and the blood gets all dry and crusty like a scab while he's asleep and then when he wakes up, he can't move like he's wearing armor and it rusted shut like the tin man in the wizard of oz. That would be cool. Just a suggestion."

Ronald tried to write another story as good as the story about the bat, but he had trouble coming up with an idea. He leafed through the *Guide* looking at photos of insects and hoping to get some inspiration, but nothing came.

Once upon a time….

That was as far as Ronald got. He stood in the window and looked out at the field. No one was playing baseball. He opened the *Guide* to the section about flies and read until he fell asleep.

It took Ronald two days to write his new story. Cook put it in an envelope and taped it to the front door.

THAT'S USING YOUR HEAD,
a story by Ronald Matthews

There are 120,000 species of flies. This is a story about one of them.

While the boy was standing waist-deep in a shallow puddle, washing the bat's blood off his arms, he heard a funny sound. He waded out of the puddle and saw something startling — the sandy ground between two blades of grass was softening and falling away. A sinkhole was forming. A shiny, black bubble the size of a baseball cap could be seen at the bottom of the hole. What was it? A balloon? The boy had an impulse to poke it with his sword (the mandible of a scimitar beetle).

Each time the balloon filled — with blood? — another six inches of it emerged from the hole. The balloon deflated and then inflated. Each time, more of it rose out of the ground. When most of the bubble was visible, two brown disks emerged, each one about the size of the boy's hand. After them came the tips of two black legs. The legs swept away grains of sand and, with a swimming motion, transferred them underground. Using this odd swimming motion, the bubble slowly ascended from the hole. At last, a withered black insect that appeared to be ten feet long, lay on the earth. Atop its shoulders was the cone-shaped balloon. Bits of sand were still clinging to its damp surface.

The creature began to groom its black bubble with its soft legs, cleaning off every particle of dirt. Eventually, the bubble gleamed in the sunlight, completely clean. When its surface was clean, the bubble began to deflate. At the same time, the withered body began to fill out. Eventually, the balloon vanished, and the two brown disks came together.

"Eyes!" the boy said out loud.

There, right in front of him, stood a fly.

This strange method of splitting its head in half and pumping its blood in and out of a bladder was the amazing method the fly used to swim from its underground pupa to the surface of the earth.

The fly carefully unfolded its wings.

"Hello," the boy said. "Nice to meet you."

The fly peered at the boy though one of her brown disks, a compound eye.

"I don't suppose you're dead?" the fly asked.

"Certainly not!"

The fly snorted. "I couldn't get more than four or five eggs into you even if you were." The fly turned away from the boy as if he was no longer worth talking to. She began to groom her right foreleg.

"I know someone who might be dead," the boy said.

The fly stopped cleaning her leg. "Does he move?"

"Not anymore."

She moved a step closer to the boy.

"Does he smell?"

The boy pinched his nose.

"He sure does!"

The fly trembled with excitement.

"Is he … big?"

"Enormous!"

The fly leapt off the ground and flew rapidly around the boy's head, landing exactly in the spot where she had begun.

"Where is he? Tell me, tell me, tell me!"

"See that shadow?" The boy pointed to a shadow that lay like a black carpet almost at their feet. It travelled overground until it arrived at the dead bat.

"Ah," said the fly. Without another word, she leapt into the air and flew at great speed to the carcass.

Hours later, the demolition of the bat was well underway. A hundred ants swarmed over the corpse. They tore off all the flesh they could hold in their jaws and ran the bits back to their nest, passed the meat into the nest, and scurried back for more.

The dead bat was hundreds of times too big to be completely devoured by a company of ants. By the afternoon of the first day, the bat's remains were the property of the flies. They clustered around the bat's soft eyes, the wet interior of its throat, and the open wound the boy had carved in its belly. One by one, they pushed themselves into these openings and sprayed their eggs over every soft thing they found.

Within two days, the maggots and ants transformed the bat into a ghost ship, flapping tattered sails, its gruesome death's head grinning blindly up at nothing.

The End.

CHAPTER 12: A POEM BY RONALD MATTHEWS

FLY,

Were I
You
And you
Me
As Fly
Would I
Satisfy?
Would I
Dare
Creep
Atop that Heap
And if I did
Would I
Care
To bend my head
And lick my shoe
As you
Do?

Cook finished reading Ronald's poem, removed her reading glasses, folded them up and put them in a pocket of her smock.

"Is the heap what I think it is?"

"What do you think?"

There was a dog that Cook hated. Every day, it entered the back yard and left a large deposit. No one in the neighborhood admitted to owning the dog. It did not wear a collar. Ronald wished it was his dog but, because of his condition, he was not allowed to have any pets, not even a fish. Cook referred to the dog as Poopsie. The moment she noticed Poopsie had again visited the yard and done his business, she went out with a plastic bag and removed the evidence. She often threatened to call Animal Control on Poopsie, but she never did. She said that people who let their dogs run around loose like that should be shot.

Using his binoculars, Ronald had inspected one of Poopsie's "heaps" and noticed the excrement had hardly left the dog's rectum before a fly appeared and wandered all over it. The sight of the intrepid fly had inspired him to write a poem.

"But do you like my poem?"

Cook said, "I have work to do. Your mother will be home for dinner."

Ronald's life had changed in a surprising way since he wrote the story about the dead bat. His mother's honeymoon had ended abruptly. She had returned in the middle of the night — without the brain surgeon. The next day, she had filed for divorce. She was already back at work, defending accused criminals. Cook and Ronald were forbidden to mention the name of the brain surgeon. It was as if he had never existed.

At night when she got home, Ronald's mother came into his room wearing a mask and protective clothing, sat beside his bed, and told him about her day.

There was only so much of this that Ronald could stand.

"What happened in LA?"

"What do you mean, darling?" his mother said.

"To the brain surgeon, Dr. Leo. Your husband."

"I'm sure he is fine, sweetie. He is very busy. And he is no longer my husband."

"Mom! What happened?"

"Darling, other people—we must learn to accommodate them. They have little foibles. You know?" Ronald had no idea what a "foible" was but decided not to ask. "They have certain habits, little tendencies that irritate. They may leave their underwear on the floor. They may snore. They may clip their toenails and leave those same toenails on the bathroom floor. We must forgive them. We all have these little irritating foibles."

"OK?" Ronald said.

"There are things, however, certain actions, certain dishonesties, that are unforgiveable." Ronald's mother sighed.

"Like what?"

Ronald's mother refused to say what the unforgiveable thing was that Dr. Leo had done. "Good night, darling."

When Ronald complained about his mother's refusal to tell him why she broke up with the brain surgeon, Cook said, "My advice, mister? Don't never mention Dr. Leo to your mother. Don't mention his pretty nurse neither. Her especially. In fact, any kind of nurse, don't mention them."

"I don't get it." Ronald stared at Cook. "Why not?"

"Never you mind, sweetie."

Ronald was very happy about the end of his mother's marriage, so happy that for an entire month he did not write any more stories.

Cook said she had heard that writers have to be miserable, or they can't write anything.

"Since your mom came home, you're too happy. You're content. That's the problem."

"Oh, what do you know?" Ronald said.

The lack of new stories was disappointing to the neighbor kids. Every few days, Mary Margaret and her friends Jan and Ann would knock on the front door and ask Cook if the sick boy had written any more stories.

"Oh, for Pete's sake, if he writes one, I'll put it out here," Cook said. "Quit bothering me."

Cook brought Ronald his lunch, sat down in the armchair, and watched him eat. "By the way, I just remembered. One of them girls left you a note. Where'd I put that?"

Dear Ronald, I have a question. In the story about the boring beetle, you mentioned a girl who rides on grasshoppers. This is what I want to know will the girl turn into an insect is she poisonous and does she smell bad because I hope not and I think you should give her a name my favorite name in the whole world is Melody. Yours truly Ann.

PS My second favorite name is Desiree.

Every day, Ronald paged through the *Guide* hoping to see a photograph that would inspire him, but nothing did. He felt it was time to do something different with his stories. But what? He read two of his old stories again and thought about recopying them because, when they had come back from his readers, they had gotten wrinkled and stained.

His main character, the boy, should turn into an insect. Obviously! But what kind? Probably he should bring back the red-haired girl, last seen flying away on the back of a grasshopper. Ronald tried to recall what exactly he had said about that girl, but the details had grown vague, and he had misplaced that particular story. Probably no one else remembered it. Besides, he was the writer! He could do anything he liked with the Grasshopper Girl. For example, he could change the color of her hair. Brown? Blue? Yellow?

Ronald sighed. Writing stories is difficult when you have too many options. He liked it better when the entire story practically wrote itself. It was like opening a door. You look through the doorway and see it — the entire story — and all you have to do is write it down. Unfortunately, sometimes you opened the door and saw — nothing.

He lay back on his bed and looked at the plastic stars on his ceiling.

A SAD STORY ABOUT AN OLD BUTTERFLY,
by Ronald Matthews

Early that morning, every plant was covered with drops of water, each one the size of the boy's head. The boy leaned close to one, saw himself on its curved surface, and bit into his own reflection. The globe exploded, splashing water all over him. That was refreshing.

Far above his head, a yellow and black garden spider had woven an enormous net. Each of its ropes (transparent twisted tubes full of glue) had become a necklace of dewdrops. Everywhere, flower-mouths began to open, revealing their pools of nectar and stalks of chewy yellow pollen. Perfumes began to drift from the flowers. Drawn by the scents, dozens of butterflies arrived.

The boy found a complicated flower that, upon inspection, turned out to be a tightly packed cluster of long, narrow flowers — a flower made of flowers. Each little flower resembled a flute and contained an ounce or two of sugary nectar. The boy drank the nectar from one little flower and then ate the petal-flesh of another.

"Delicious!"

A White Cabbage butterfly landed heavily upon a pink flower-cluster several yards away from the boy. In the edge of one of her wings was a beak-shaped gash. She was missing so many scales on another of her wings that in places it had become transparent. She opened and closed her wings and began to crawl over the pink cluster, flicking her proboscis into each flower and occasionally hiccoughing.

"Good morning," the boy said.

The butterfly's head came out of the flower.

"Hic! What'd yuh want? You wouldn't wanna eat an old girl, would you?"

"Certainly not. Especially not one so pretty as you."

"Well, a lady can't be too careful." Examining the boy through her compound eyes, the butterfly opened and closed her wings. "See yuh, baby." Unsteadily, she climbed to the edge of the cluster and sprang into the air. She ascended in a zigzag until she collided with the lower edge of the garden spider's web.

"Oh, dear," the boy said.

From the center of the web, a taut rope extended at an angle to a tree branch. Every movement of the butterfly caused this rope to tremble.

A black leg appeared and carefully felt the trembling line. After a moment, the yellow-striped garden spider tiptoed rapidly down the tightrope. She paused to peer at her captive. Seeing that the butterfly was defenseless, she sprang atop the insect and nipped her. After tying up the butterfly, she dragged her to the center of the net, where she tore off the wings and threw them out of the web. They spiraled down and landed a few feet away from the boy.

The End

Cook read this story and returned it to Ronald without any comment.

Ronald said, "You like it?"

"I'd like it better if it had a happy ending," Cook said.

"Sometimes you are so irritating!" Ronald said.

CHAPTER 13: THE GIRL WITH BLACK AND WHITE HAIR, A STORY BY RONALD MATTHEWS

The girl was riding on top of her grasshopper. She had weird hair. Her hair was pure white on one side and black on the other side. She and her hopper were skimming over the grass forest because she was looking for her father, the famous entomologist Dr. Henry Fabber, who had gone missing and was believed dead. The Girl with Black and White Hair did not believe her dad was dead. She believed he was down here in the grass forest doing research on the lifestyles of insects and spiders, research he would write up for his next book. This new book would be called *The Intelligent Girl's Guide to Insects and Spiders*. When finished, it would be fatter than the earlier book, *The Boy's Guide*, and have lots more photographs. The girl had a theory about why her dad was down there in the grass forest.

While she was skimming above the forest, the girl did not see any sign of her dad, but she did notice a boy stuck in a spider's web. Probably he was blown there by a gust of breeze. He didn't look happy. The spider was spinning him around and around and wrapping him in silk.

"Time to go to work," she told her hopper, who zoomed close to the spider's web. Gripping her sword, Stinger, the girl jumped off her hopper and landed on the web, not far from the spider and the boy. She did not get stuck because she knew a thing or two about spider-rope. Each rope is actually three strands braided together. Only one of these contains glue. It's possible to run along a rope and not get stuck if you are careful never to step on one of the sticky strands. This requires skill, but the girl was up to the job.

The spider was outraged by the fact that a girl was in its web and would have attacked her, except she kept poking at it with her sword. The spider let go of the boy and retreated. It preferred prey that did not have a sword. Spiders that spin webs are not very brave. They like their prey to get tangled in the sticky web. Then the spider can come down its rope, avoiding the sticky strands, and capture the prey without any trouble. The girl was not cooperating. She was acting more like a predator than prey.

When the spider was a safe distance away, the girl cut the boy loose. He fell out of the web and landed hard on the ground. The girl balanced on a rope, one of the non-sticky ones, like a tightrope walker, and looked down at the boy.

"Hey, kid? You OK?"

The boy was sprawled on the ground beneath the web. He was not moving.

"You dead?"

The girl put two of her fingers in her mouth and whistled, which was the signal to her hopper to come get her. Grasshoppers can hear because they are one of the noise-making insects. The hopper glided past, and the girl jumped from the web right onto its back. She had excellent balance.

The hopper landed on the ground beside the boy, and the girl jumped off.

"Hey!" she yelled. "Wake up!" The girl hoped she had not broken the boy. Maybe the fall had knocked him unconscious. He was lying on his side, not saying anything, but at least he did not seem to be bleeding. She wondered if the spider had bitten him.

"Wow, kid, I hate to say it," the girl said, "but you stink."

This particular boy was poisonous. The spider probably would never have eaten him. If it had, it would have gotten sick and died.

"You gonna get up, or what?" The girl nudged the boy with her toe.

"No," the boy said. "Leave me alone."

The girl and the boy had met before.

"I can't keep saving you," the girl said. "You need to start watching where you're going."

The boy stood up and brushed off some spider web that was stuck to his pajamas. He knew he ought to say thank you to the girl for saving his life, but he was in a bad mood. He didn't think she was very nice, talking about how he smelled. It wasn't his fault he stank. He had been cursed by an evil wizard. Besides, if he didn't stink of poison, he would get eaten. The girl didn't stink because she was not poisonous. She was wearing a magic suit that made her invulnerable. Lucky her. She could probably fall out of a spider's web and not get hurt one little bit, but he was shaken up by his fall and probably bruised. Also, his left shoulder blade itched.

"You haven't seen my dad, have you?" The girl said her name was Melody Desiree Fabber. She said she had been down here in the grass forest for weeks, looking for her dad, the famous entomologist Henry Fabber. So far, she had not found hide nor hair of him. A lot of girls might have gotten discouraged when faced with a predicament like this one, but not Melody Desiree Fabber. She knew the importance of maintaining a positive attitude.

The boy scratched his shoulder blade. He wished the girl with black and white hair would stop talking. He got to his knees and stood up.

The girl had a theory about her dad. She was pretty sure he had contacted the wizard when he found out the wizard could shrink people. Lots of people might think that a terrible fate, getting shrunk and left in the grass forest where you could be eaten by a predatory insect or a spider, but Dr. Fabber loved insects and spiders. He studied them and wrote books about them. Most people would hate the very thought of getting shrunk until you were no bigger than an ant, but not Dr. Fabber. He would love the opportunity. What better way to study insects than to meet them face to face? The girl's theory was that her dad had made a deal with the wizard, and the wizard had shrunk him. But something had gone wrong.

Now that he had had time to recover from his fall, the boy started feeling better about the girl. Maybe she did talk too much about his smell, but before she appeared, the spider had been wrapping him up like a mummy.

"Thanks," he said.

"For what?"

"For saving me from that darn spider. I might have been hung up in that web for who knows how long? Swinging in the wind like a wind chime until I starved to death."

"You woulda died of thirst first."

"Well, thanks again. And no, I haven't seen any sign of your dad."

The boy decided he admired Melody Desiree Fabber's hair which was white on one side and black on the other, parted in the middle. Why should a girl have one color hair when she can have two colors? Also, he wished he had a cool sword like she had. Her sword even had a name, Stinger. Like right now, talking to her, he wished he had a sword to wave around. That would be wicked cool. The boy thought about getting a stick or something and waving it, but a stick would never be as cool as a sword. Not to mention she had a suit that made her invulnerable. The boy thought that, if the girl would just shut up about his smell, she would be almost perfect.

While the boy was thinking, the girl was explaining why she knew her dad must be down here in the forest.

Before he had disappeared, her father had left her a note. The note said:

Have chance to study insects and spiders up close and personal will be gone two weeks if you need me contact the wizard.

"I don't trust that wizard," the boy said. It was the same wizard who had shrunk him. And for what? All he had done was compare the wizard's nose to a potato. Now his other shoulder blade itched, so he gave it a good scratch.

The girl said it was pretty obvious what had happened. Her father must have made a bargain with the wizard. The deal was the wizard would shrink him, and Dr. Fabber could spend 14 days down here in the grass forest studying the lifestyles of insects and spiders. Then, the 14 days came and went. When Dr. Fabber did not return, Melody got worried. After the 16th day came and went, she went to the wizard's house and pounded on his door. When the wizard cracked open the door and looked at her, she demanded to know where her father was. The wizard denied any responsibility. He claimed he'd never heard of any Doctor Fabber. He suggested she check the morgue. The wizard slammed his door right in her face.

"Rude," the boy said. "What'd you do?" He wished he had not scratched his shoulder blade with his fingernails because now it itched worse than ever.

That night, when the wizard was sound asleep, the girl broke into his house. She did not literally have to break in because there was a window not quite shut. She got it open and climbed into his kitchen. Luckily, the wizard did not have a dog to warn him because dogs hate wizards. Everyone knows that. While he was sound asleep and snoring, the girl investigated the wizard's house and finally entered his bedroom. That took bravery, you better believe it, because what if he woke up?

The boy said, "His ring! How'd you get his magic ring? Wasn't it on his finger?"

The girl said the magic ring was lying on a little bedside table.

"Can I see it?" the boy asked. His shoulders were itching like the devil.

"You can look at it, but don't you dare touch it." Melody held out her hand and displayed the ring, which she was wearing on her thumb. "Take a look at the ruby and the magical inscriptions." She explained that, at night, the wizard had to take the ring off when he was sleeping because a magic ring could get activated accidentally. If, for example, the wizard rolled over in his bed and unconsciously rubbed the ring in exactly the right way, who knows what might happen? He might turn into a toad. Everyone knows nothing is more dangerous than a magic ring when it is accidentally activated. It is just common sense.

Melody said, "I notice you are looking at my Suit of Invulnerability. You are probably wondering where I got it."

That night, when Melody had got hold of the ring, she tiptoed out of the wizard's bedroom. She carried the ring into the kitchen where the light was better because the moonlight was streaming in through the window, the same window she had crawled through to get into the wizard's house. The ring's red ruby glowed like fire in the moonlight, and she had an idea. She knew the wizard must have a magic suit because how else could he wander around in the grass forest and not get eaten? It was just common sense. She spoke to the ring.

"Wow," the boy said. In his imagination, he could see the girl holding the ring and the red ruby glowing like fire in the moonlight. "I never would have thought of that." His admiration for her increased.

Melody asked the magic ring to direct her to the suit. She turned in a circle. "That's why the ring led me in the right direction. When I was facing the correct way, the ring began to glow, and every time I took a step in the right direction, the red ruby glowed brighter. It was guiding me, see? Every time I took a step in the right direction, it glowed brighter and brighter until I was standing in front of a closet. I pulled the closet door open, and guess what, the magic suit was hanging inside the closet on a hanger. The wizard's magic sword was there too, standing up in a corner. I put the ring on. It was too big for my ring finger, so I put it on my thumb. Then I started to get a feeling, know what I mean? I took the suit off the hanger and pulled it on. It was way too big for me of course. I had to roll up the legs and the arms. The wizard was taller than me and a whole lot fatter. You better believe it. I rolled up the pantlegs and turned back the sleeves. The whole time, the ruby glowed so bright I could hardly look at it and not get blinded. I held the sword in one hand and the ring in the other and said, 'Hey, magic ring! Where's my father? Take me to my father! Now!" And then, I got all woozy and dizzy and blacked out."

"Wow," the boy said. "What happened?"

"Next thing I knew, I was down here in the forest. I was no more than an inch tall, but at least I was still wearing this magic suit, which now fits me perfectly. Because, you know, it's magic, so it adjusts. I've been looking for my dad ever since. The only bad thing is this darn ring won't work anymore."

The boy said he wished he could help her with her missing dad problem, but he hadn't seen Dr. Fabber. His shoulder blades were itching so bad he was having trouble paying attention.

The girl replied that she had no doubt her father was down here, somewhere nearby, but where? She confessed her worst fear was that her father had been captured by ants and was being held prisoner at the bottom of an ant nest because, if that was the case, how would she ever find him? "There are hundreds of ant nests down here. Maybe thousands."

"Please excuse me," the boy said. "It's just I've got this terrible itch. Don't mind me. I have to scratch, or I'm gonna die!" He unbuttoned his pajama top so he could give himself a tremendous scratch. Both his shoulders were driving him insane. It was as if they were on fire.

"Uh-oh. A really bad itch?" Melody asked. "I bet I know what your problem is."

She walked around the boy so she could take a look at his shoulders. Each shoulder blade was adorned with a big red bump, the cause of all the itching.

"Yup," Melody said. "It's just like I thought. You're growing wings. You're turning into an insect!"

CHAPTER 14: FAN MAIL

Cook brought in the mail, which included a letter from Max and a letter from Mary Margaret.

Hey, Buddy! What's up? I read your story. Pretty crazy he's turning into a bug. I hope he turns into a bee and stings the wizard on his big fat nose. You should name the boy in your stories. You should name him Max because Max is a strong name. You should make him more of a badass. It's stupid when the girl has to save him all the time. If he's going to be weak and need to be rescued a lot then don't call him Max because I would not be like that. What you should do is get rid of the grasshopper girl. Replace her with a guy who could be the boy's best friend. Then me and the boy should go kill the wizard and save all the people who got turned into bugs. Don't take advice from my sister because she is stupid. She will just try to get you to turn your story into a love story which would ruin it. Your friend, MAX

Dear Ronald, I don't understand why the girl character, the one who rides grasshoppers no longer has red hair like me. She used to have red hair. Red hair is a lot better than black and white hair. Also, in the new story you say the boy wishes he had a sword, but he did have one. You probably forgot. In the story about the bat, he used a scimitar beetle's mandible to cut his way out of the stomach of the bat. I hope you correct these mistakes as soon as possible. How are you feeling? Sincerely, Mary Margaret.

The next day, Cook brought in a letter from Max's sister Ann. Ann must have worked harder on this letter because it included punctuation.

Dear Ronald, I and my friend Jan love the name Melody Desiree but not the last name Fabber which sounds sort of silly. Me and Jan think it's really cool how the girl has white hair on one side and black on the other, because I have dark hair which is almost black and Jan has blond hair which is almost white. My mom who is a hair stylist says you can't really have two color hair naturally unless you got a head injury so probably the girl is dying half her hair black and bleaching half white. A young girl should not be using bleach and dye when she is so young because it could damage her hair and this is why me and Jan wonder if the girl has a good hair stylist or is she doing it herself? We think the boy is already starting to fall in love with the girl but our brothers say the boy is too young to fall in love. How old is he anyway? We think he could be 13 or even 14. And what is his name? It is really starting to bother us that he doesn't have a name but please don't call him Max or Josh because those are stupid names. The boy needs to figure out how to defeat the wizard and save his mom because didn't you say in an earlier story the wizard is trying to get the boy's mom to marry him so he can get all her money? The boy should quit exploring the forest and meeting more bugs and get to work saving his mom from the wizard. Also he should help Melody find her missing father. If they work together on a mystery that would make it easier for them to fall in love. And what about winter, have you thought about winter? When it gets cold at night, all the bugs will die, so the boy and Melody better find Dr. Fabber and grow big again before winter comes. We like it that the boy is growing wings and hope he turns into a butterfly. We think monarchs are the best, they are the big ones with orange and black wings. Did you know that monarchs fly south, they migrate to Mexico for the winter, so the boy could turn into one and not die when it gets cold. But if he flies south to Mexico, how is he ever going to find Dr. Fabber and save his mom from the wizard? We love your stories and hope they get better. Yours Truly, Ann.

PS Jan helped me write this. She says hi too.

***

Cook said, "You look pale. I better take your temperature." She stuck a thermometer in Ronald's mouth.

Ronald thought about the letters. He felt they should contain more praise and fewer criticisms. He thought Max and Ann and Mary Margaret should write their own stories if they knew so much. He wished he had thought about winter and what it does to insects. He had never once thought about winter. Now, what was he going to do? What about the Luna moth? She had claimed to be hundreds of years old! Obviously, that was not going to work. He wished he had not said the boy was growing wings. Now he was going to have to decide what sort of insect the boy would turn into. He decided the boy was not going to turn into a bee or a butterfly. Definitely not. But what else could he turn into? And what was the boy's name? He had no idea.

"I better check your blood pressure, too." Cook wrapped a blood pressure sleeve around Ronald's arm.

Maybe not all the insects should talk, just the ones cursed by the wizard. The others could be normal, non-speaking insects. The talking ones could survive the winter if they sneaked into someone's warm house or hibernated or something like that.

"A common house fly," Ronald said. "Did you know they have five eyes? Two compound eyes and three simple eyes."

"What's that, honey?" Cook stepped back and looked at Ronald. His eyes were glazed, and his cheeks were turning bright red. "Oh, my goodness!" Cook said.

Ronald said, "Soon, I will have a grey body with four black lines on my thorax."

Cook said, "Oh no, oh no, oh no."

"My entire body, even my abdomen, will be covered with hair," Ronald whispered. "I will grow one pair of membranous wings."

"Oh, my poor sweet darling," Cook said. "Hold on, hold on, hold on."

Ronald did not say anything else for a long time.

CHAPTER 15: THE WATER STRIDER

Ronald did not get to enjoy his fourteenth birthday because at the time he was in an induced coma, attended by nurses wearing zippered coveralls, gloves, masks, and goggles. Every evening after work, his mother came to the hospital with her files about her clients, the accused criminals. She studied them in the waiting room, sometimes getting up to look through the little window at Ronald. She noticed that he moved his arms and legs but never opened his eyes. The nurses said Ronald was having dreams, a good sign. They said his heartbeat and blood pressure had stabilized, but they were worried about his temperature.

Ronald was dreaming that he was the boy in his stories. The boy was hot, very hot, and there were itchy bumps on his forehead. Itchy bumps on his shoulder blades and similar bumps on his forehead. And he was so darn hot! It was early morning, but already it was so hot that all he wanted to do was lie down and sleep. Something told him it might be dangerous to fall asleep. There were so many predators around.

The boy was standing at the edge of a pond full to the brim with cool dirty water. He was so hot! He would dearly love to jump in! But he had better be careful. A pond like that was probably inhabited by water striders and dragonfly nymphs. The nymphs were especially terrifying. You couldn't see them. They lurked just under the surface of the water. Each one was equipped with an extensible lower lip, if you could call it a lip, attached to its chin, if you could call it a chin. The creatures kept their extendable lips tucked under their chests and, if any delicious prey appeared, the lip would shoot out and GRAB the prey.

At least, you could see the water striders. There was one, right there, floating half-submerged in the water.

It was so darn hot! The boy's head hurt, and his shoulders itched. Oh, if only he could wade into the dirty water of the pond and cool off! That would be wonderful. Maybe water striders are not as dangerous as people say.

The strider's bifocal eyes peered at the boy. It floated closer to him. The upper halves of its eyes were above the water and could inspect the boy. The lower halves gazed down into the watery world below the strider. The strider floated a little closer.

As the sun rose higher into the sky, and the day grew even hotter, the boy noticed that a hundred miniature reflections of himself danced in the facets of the strider's eye.

It was a hot morning, and it was going to get worse. The boy wondered if maybe he could just dip his bare feet into the cool water of the pool. But that strider was worrisome.

The moment the boy moved a step closer to the pond, the strider pulled itself up out of the water. It spun around and ran atop the water until it stood still, balanced on six dimples of water. It was VERY close to the boy now. Too close!

The boy took a step back. And another step. And another. He did not want to be anywhere near the grasp of the strider's long front legs.

"Don't mind me!" the strider said. It spun around twice and tiptoed backwards, balancing on top of the surface tension of the water. "It's awfully hot, isn't it? I don't know how you can stand it. Good day for a dip. A nice cool dip will cool you right off! Come on in, my sweet."

"I don't know," the boy replied. The water did look invitingly cool. "I think I'll just stay right here."

The strider skated closer to the boy.

"Perhaps you would like to try walking on the water?" It spun in a circle. "Do you see? So easy! All you have to do is step lightly. Very, very lightly. You can do that, can't you?"

"You certainly make it look easy," the boy said.

"Oh, it is easy! So easy! Try it! Just, ah, step down. The water will hold you up! Don't worry."

"I suppose, if I fall in, you'll take my hand?"

"It would be an honor!" The strider got so excited, it spun around six times. "Here!" It extended one of its long front legs. "Let me help you!"

The boy looked down at the dirty water and shook his head. "That particular patch of water looks soft. I don't think it would hold me."

"Hold you? Of course, it will! Look how it holds me!" The strider spun in a circle on top of the water. "It's hard! Wonderfully, horribly hard!" The strider jumped up and down, causing little dimples and wavelets of water to scramble away in every direction as if fleeing for their lives.

"Maybe you are right about that particular patch of water right there, but I don't think it's nearly as hard over there."

"THAT water," the strider declared, "is even harder! Look how hard!" It pounced upon the indicated spot, causing it to tremble so violently that, in the water below the strider, the insect's reflection appeared to be trying desperately to pull loose and escape.

"You certainly are convincing, but I wonder if you would mind showing me that all the rest of the pond is firm? It would put my mind so much more at ease. Maybe you could just run back and forth over all the water between me and that reed over there." The boy pointed at a large plant growing up out of the water.

"Oh, is that all? And after I run over there, after I show you how HARD the water is, you'll step right down, won't you, dear? You'll step onto the water? I'll help you!"

"Oh yes, just run all the way over to that reed and back, and I'll be convinced. Unless of course you're afraid of falling through. I wouldn't want you to hurt yourself."

"Hurt myself?! Fall through?! I'll show you who falls through!"

The strider danced atop the water so rapidly and frantically it made the boy almost dizzy to watch. At last, the strider arrived at the reed, where it was promptly seized by a dragonfly nymph and eaten.

When at last Ronald came back to life, he told his mother the story of the water strider. He told his mom, "When I had the dream about the strider, I believed I was the boy in my stories. I was so hot. My forehead ached and my shoulders ached. Everything hurt. I wanted to jump into the pond even though I knew how dangerous it was. I was so tired and hot. I wanted to, Mommy. I wanted to jump in. I didn't care anymore. But I didn't. Are you happy I didn't jump in, Mommy?"

"I love you very much, darling," Ronald's mother said. She wanted to hug him, but she was wearing protective clothing and hugging was not allowed.

"I love you so very, very much!"

CHAPTER 16: JUST LIKE ICE CREAM

That fall, when Ronald returned to his room, waiting for him was another large present from his father, *The Collected Works of Charles Dickens*. Ronald spent his days reading Dickens and looking out his window. Most days, there was nothing much to see, but on weekends, the neighbor kids still congregated in the field outside Ronald's window. They no longer played baseball. Now, they played flag football.

Ronald watched and soon had many questions. The boys would get into two lines and face one another. Then there was lots of shoving. One kid was behind one of the lines. He had a ball— a weirdly shaped one with pointy ends. Usually, he threw the ball, but sometimes he gave the ball to someone else. More shoving. After a while, the two lines formed again. Ronald said, "I'm pretty sure the object is to snatch the handkerchief out of that one boy's back pocket. That handkerchief must be what they call the flag. I get that part, but that's about all I get."

Cook said the rules of flag football are impossibly complicated and no one her age could possibly remember them.

Cook must have told Ronald's mother about his interest because that evening, his mom gave him a list of flag football rules (prepared by her secretary). Ronald studied the rules but soon had lots more questions.

"What does forward pass mean? What is the line of scrimmage? What is a handoff exactly? What is the rusher? What does 'loss of down' mean? What does it mean when it says the ball is 'dead' when it touches the ground? Balls aren't alive, how can they be dead?"

Cook said, "Beats me. You hungry?"

After studying the rules for hours, Ronald announced he agreed with Cook; the rules of flag football are so complicated they are impossible to understand. He watched the boys play their game anyway. Sometimes he saw Max and Josh out there, but they never came up to his window to say hi. They didn't even look in his direction.

Cook said, "Them kids can't come around so much because they're back at school."

Ronald said, "What is that like exactly, school?"

Cook said, "It's no fun. You wouldn't like it."

Hoping to get his mind off the neighbor kids, Cook told Ronald that while he was in the hospital, the entire house was fumigated. An exterminator sprayed insecticide everywhere. The whole house reeked for 24 hours. Cook said, "After the exterminator left, dozens of them centipedes staggered out of the basement walls and died in the middle of the floor. I had to sweep them up. Yuck! I should have called up that darn exterminator and made him do it. I hate them centipedes with a passion."

Ronald turned away from the window but didn't say anything.

Cook said she was still interested in the stories about Insect Boy, even if they were horror stories. "Did that boy turn into a grasshopper, or a bumble bee, or what? Hey, you ought to write a story about them centipedes. Good subject for you. I mean, if you wanna write another story."

"A grasshopper? Of course not. Why would you even think he would turn into one? Or a bumble bee? Don't be stupid."

The next morning, Ronald was hard at work on another story.

FLY BOY,
a story by Ronald Matthews

The boy grew antennae out of his forehead. His wings emerged from his shoulder blades and dried. And then, one night when he was asleep, everything changed, his entire body sprouted hair. When he woke up, his legs and arms had turned into four skinny black hairy legs, and he had grown two extra legs. Six legs. He had turned into a common housefly! Except he still had his human head. It had two antennae, the short stubby kind.

Melody inspected the boy's new body and said she was not impressed. She told the boy he'd better watch out for spiders because, if there's anything spiders love to eat, it's flies. She was lucky she had the suit of invulnerability because otherwise she too would have turned into an insect. Her magic suit saved her from that horrible fate.

In other ways, Melody's life was not that great. She still had no idea how to use her magic ring. She figured she must have broken it. At least she still had power over grasshoppers. All she had to do was snap her fingers and a hopper showed up to give her a ride. She was getting discouraged because no matter how hard she looked, she couldn't find her father, the famous entomologist Henry Fabber. Plus, it was starting to get cold at night.

"And you know what that means."

"What's it mean?" the boy asked. He had just discovered he had pads and claws on his feet. He also discovered he could taste things just by walking over them.

"It means we better sneak into somebody's warm house, or we'll die."

The boy figured they had a few weeks left before it got that cold. Besides, he wanted to work on his flying. Flying was harder than it looked. Lots harder. He kept crashing.

Melody said, "Your trouble is you think too much. Just fly!"

Ronald picked up his telephone and rapped on the window of his door until Cook appeared and picked up her telephone.

"What is it, honey?"

"Writing stories is too hard."

Cook said, "What's the problem? Maybe I can help."

"I doubt it. I'm trying to imagine what it's like to be a house fly."

"What's so hard about that? You fly around the house, buzzing. Watch out for fly swatters."

"That is an ignorant comment and shows how little you know about anything. Besides, he's outdoors."

"OK, smartie pants, tell me what it's like."

"The boy is especially worried about spider webs."

"Sounds right."

"I bet you didn't know spiders make webs on top of the grass. I've seen them with my binoculars. You can see them in the morning because of the dew. That's the ONLY time you can see them. Then they become invisible."

Cook looked confused. "Invisible spiders?"

"I don't even know why I talk to you. The *webs* become invisible!"

Since he came home from the hospital, Ronald's conversations with Cook were limited in duration because she was no longer allowed to remain in his room for long, even if she was wearing protective clothing and a mask. The doctors were worried about what might happen if anyone breathed on Ronald. Cook hated the suit and the mask; she over-heated wearing them, but she hated it even more that she could not spend much time with Ronald.

Fortunately, while Ronald was in the hospital, his room had been equipped with a telephone. Cook could pick up a telephone on her side of the door and Ronald could pick up the telephone on his side of the door. They could see one another through the window in the door. They could look at one another and talk, but never touch.

Ronald said, "It's probably hard to learn to fly. And then, if you ALSO have to worry about invisible spider webs, it's super hard!"

Cook recalled when she learned to drive. She said, now she thought about it, she did remember sometimes seeing spider webs on top of the lawn grass, sparkling with dew drops. "You can see them in the early morning, but—"

"Exactly. Then the dew evaporates, and you can't see them anymore. They become invisible. Don't you see? The boy needs to *practice* flying, but he's scared to because what if he crash-lands and winds up tangled in one of those invisible spider webs?"

Cook said, "You could draw pictures. I mean, if you hate writing stories, stop, take a break, just draw pictures for a while. Or you could read. You love reading. I can't believe you've read all those fat books your dad sent you."

In fact, Ronald was only halfway through the first one which was about a fat man named Mr. Pickwick and his friends.

"Or you could do your exercises."

Ronald was supposed to do exercises every day. Ten pushups, ten sit ups, ten jumping jacks, ten leg lifts, and then run-in-place for five minutes. He especially hated the leg lifts.

Cook said the boy in the story would probably have to learn to see again.

"Because didn't you say, since he's turned into a fly, he has five eyes, not normal eyes, five weird insect eyes?"

"Do you even listen? I just told you he still has his regular head."

On the other side of the door, Cook rubbed her chin.

"So, he still has normal eyes, human eyes. That's good. But what about his antennas? What exactly do you do with antennas anyway?"

"He is flooded with smells, all kinds of smells."

"You know what? I just had an idea. This is kind of yucky, but also funny. Dog poop."

"What about it?"

"Flies love dog poop—like that poem you wrote. If he's a fly, wouldn't he be attracted to fresh poop? He's flying around like you said, wiggling his antennas, and then he smells some brand-new poop and—oh my goodness gracious! —he has to go there right away! To him, poop smells just like ice cream."

"Oh, go away. You're giving me a headache." Ronald hung up his telephone.

Cook peeked in at Ronald half an hour later and smiled to herself because Ronald was working on his story again.

FLY BOY (CONTINUED),
by Ronald Matthews

Melody couldn't give the boy flying lessons since she didn't have wings. Her flying was accomplished for her by grasshoppers. The boy tried asking one of her grasshoppers for advice, but instead of saying anything, the hopper spat at him.

Teaching himself to fly was dangerous. One time, the boy almost flew into a web, the kind that is laid upon the surface of the grass and is invisible except in the morning when it is lined with dew drops. The boy was so scared of those webs that he dared to fly only in the early morning.

When he was not terrified about getting caught in a web or crashing, the boy liked flying. In fact, at times, flying was pretty great. It was wonderful to be balancing on a breeze with the whole forest down below.

Unfortunately, he could never relax even when he was high up in the air. Why? Birds. Some of them swoop down like fighter planes and eat insects. There is even a horrible insect-eating bird known as the Flycatcher. They are the worst! And the hummingbirds are almost as bad. Who knew hummingbirds can catch and swallow insects in midair? The boy was terrified of again getting trapped inside the belly of a bird. That would be horrible. But, at the moment, he seemed to have the sky to himself. He flew in big lazy circles, higher and higher. Far below, the grass forest dwindled until it almost looked like what it was, a back yard. The boy was getting tired and decided he'd better come in for a landing, and then he noticed something—something much more enormous and terrifying than a spider, or even a hummingbird.

The evil wizard!

The wizard was on his hands and knees, crawling around in his back yard with a magnifying glass looking for something. Oh, my goodness, the boy realized, he must be looking for Melody, the girl who stole his magic ring and his magic suit and his sword. Without his magic ring, the wizard was unable to do magic. He was desperate to find the girl and get his magical equipment back.

The boy buzzed over the wizard's bald head. He wished he had turned into a hornet because he would love to sting the wizard on his fat sweaty neck. He landed on the wizard's back and clung to his damp shirt.

Ronald sighed. He was getting hand cramp from writing too fast. He laid down his pencil and wiggled his fingers. Now what? He had no idea what would happen next. Did the wizard notice the boy crawling on him, or not? Maybe the wizard could catch the boy, but how? Maybe he would just swat at the boy with his hand. The boy could fly away, but the wizard would notice him, a fly with the head of a boy!

Then, what would happen?

When Ronald got stuck, he hated having to think and think. Cook was right. He thought too much. Better to do exercises. Ronald did five jumping jacks and ran in place for two minutes, and sure enough, he got an idea.

Centipedes!

CHAPTER 17: THE MAN IN THE JAR

Max rang the doorbell. When Cook answered, he asked if Ronald had written any more stories. He said his sister Ann was sick with a bad cold. "Mom's making her stay home till she gets better. She's really bored, and she'd like to read one. Her favorite kind is horror."

"I'll ask him," Cook said. "You wait here on the porch."

THE SOLE SURVIVOR,
a story by Ronald Matthews

A black truck pulled up in front of the wizard's house. On the side of the truck was a sign that said BOB THE EXTERMINATOR, PEST CONTROL OUR SPECIALITY. A fat man wearing a cap got out of his truck, opened the back end, and hauled out his equipment. He strapped a cannister of poison to his back and put on a face mask.

The wizard opened his front door and motioned for Bob the Exterminator to come inside.

Bob went down into the wizard's basement and sprayed poison into every hole and crack. Ten minutes later, a hundred centipedes staggered out of the walls. Every single one of those wretched creatures zigzagged to the middle of the basement floor and died!

Some people think centipedes are insects, but actually they are arthropods. Insects have three body segments and three pairs of legs. Centipedes can have lots more segments and each one comes with its own pair of legs.

Of all the centipedes that lived down in the wizard's basement, only one survived. This particular centipede had 13 segments and 26 legs. It was pure luck he survived. When the clouds of poison gas poured through the wall, the centipede just happened to be turned in the right direction. He ran as fast as he could to get away from the nasty fumes. Somehow, running as fast as he could—and take my word for it, those centipedes can run! —he got out of the basement, out of the house, and found himself in the grass forest. It was too bright out here. Much too bright. Like all centipedes, he hated light. He didn't have any eyes, but he could feel the horrible sunlight burning his skin. He wanted to find a nice dark hole and hide before a giant bird could notice him.

When Bob finished spraying poison into every corner and crack of the wizard's house, the wizard paid him in cash.

"I want you to come back here every month."

"You bet," Bob said.

Ever since the girl Melody, the daughter of Henry Fabber the famous entomologist, had stolen his magic ring, the wizard had lived in fear of insects. Every morning, as soon as he got out of bed, he rubbed himself with stinky insect repellent. He rubbed the smelly ointment on his arms and legs, on his fat stomach, and even onto his bald head, but he was still worried. He had turned lots of innocent people into insects. Maybe they would want revenge. He had to be careful. He had to find that girl and get back his ring! Every spare moment, the wizard was out in his back yard, crawling on his hands and knees with his magnifying glass, looking for the girl. When he found her, he was going to retrieve his ring and then kill her!

You are probably wondering why the ring doesn't work anymore? After she stole it, Melody used it to find the wizard's magic suit and sword and to shrink herself. That night, inside the wizard's house, the ring worked fine. All Melody had to do was tell it to do something, and the magic happened. She climbed into the magic suit which, at the time, was too big for her. In a loud voice, she said, "Magic Ring, shrink me! Now!" The ring's ruby glowed bright red, so bright it was hard to look at it and not get blinded. Melody got dizzy and then she passed out. When she woke up, she was in the grass forest and the suit fit her perfectly.

Since arriving in the grass forest, Melody had been looking for her dad but had not found him. She often spoke to the ring. "Where's my dad, Mister Ring? Take me to Dr. Fabber! I mean it!" No matter what she told the ring to do, nothing happened. "Grow me, make me big, make me tall again, enlarge me, make me normal! Unshrink me, you stupid stubborn ring!" The ring ignored her. She tried flattery. "Nice ring! Awesome and beautiful ring! Where's my dad?" Flattery proved useless. She tried threats. "If you don't take me to my father, I will STOMP on you!" She sang to the ring and kissed it. Nothing. The ring's stone never began to glow like it did when she first put it on her thumb. Melody remained tiny but at least wearing the suit, which now fit perfectly, she was invulnerable.

Also, she had power over grasshoppers. That was good. All she had to do was whistle and one showed up.

That afternoon, the boy and Melody were perched in the branches of a bush. "What is that thing?" the boy asked. He had recently finished turning into a common house fly—almost finished. He still had his human head. He had been buzzing around the grass forest all day and was now resting.

"It's a centipede," Melody said. "I hate them."

"Can it jump up here and get us?"

"I think there's something wrong with it."

The centipede did not have any eyes, but its antennae were wiggling.

The boy said, "You think it can smell us up here? Maybe we should climb higher."

When the boy had first come to the grass forest, he had been a normal-looking boy, but he had not smelled normal because the evil wizard had cursed him and made him poisonous. As a result, he stank. The other insects, even the spiders, would not dare eat him. But something had happened to him when he transformed into a common house fly. He quit stinking. It was a good change in a way. He no longer had to hear Melody complaining about his smell. The bad aspect of it was that since he was no longer poisonous, he had to worry about being grabbed and eaten—by a centipede, for example.

Melody said, "Weird that it's outdoors during the day. Normally they live in dark, damp basements. They hate sunlight."

Ronald remembered seeing the exterminator's van in the wizard's driveway. He had been flying above the wizard's house at the time. Since his first attempts when he had turned into a house fly, the boy was getting pretty good at flying. He had two wings (flies have only two wings, not four) and six legs, an abdomen, and a thorax, but his head was the same as usual, except now it had antennae, the short stubby kind.

Melody said, "They're dangerous predators full of venom. They eat anything they can grab, so be careful. Don't get too close. Hey there, Mr. Centipede, how you doing? You don't look so good."

The centipede told them the horrifying story of what had happened down in the basement. "I'm the sole survivor," he said. He coughed and trembled. "Is it cold out here? I feel cold all over."

The boy looked at Melody, and Melody looked at the boy.

"Is one of you named Melody?" the centipede asked. "I got a message for a girl named Melody."

Melody said, "That's me!"

"There's a human man in a jar down there in the basement," the centipede said. "He wants you to come save him."

"A man?" Melody said. The boy grabbed hold of her arm because he feared she might climb down, get too close to the centipede, who was after all pretty darn dangerous, even if it did look sick. "What man? Did he have a beard?"

"Watch out for the cat," the centipede said. That was the very last thing it said.

"Cat?" the boy said. "The wizard has a cat?"

The centipede coughed again and then fell over on its side. Its 26 legs jerked and trembled and then grew still.

"It's my dad!" Melody said. "It has to be! We have to go save him! We have to sneak into the wizard's house!"

Every morning, Ronald asked Cook if the neighbor girl Ann had returned his story about the sole survivor, and every day Cook said no.

"She probably has other stuff to do. Like homework. Who knows if she's even read your story yet? Maybe her stupid brother forgot to give it to her. You're so impatient!"

After five days, Ronald's story was returned with a letter. Ronald read the letter six times.

Dear Ronald, I like it that the boy no longer smells bad. I don't like it that he turned into a fly. I recommend you change that. How are they going to invade the wizard's house? Melody could sneak in because she has the magic suit, but is she vulnerable to poison? Because if she is, how can either one of them get into the house and not die? I don't understand why the ring doesn't work anymore. You need to explain that better. I have some more questions. If Dr. Fabber is trapped in a jar, how come he doesn't starve to death? Why doesn't the wizard just kill him? I don't really understand why the wizard shrinks so many people. What did they ever do to him? And what about their families, their wives and husbands and their kids? Aren't their relatives looking for them? Not to mention the police? It sounds like half the neighborhood must be missing. Wouldn't everyone be talking about it? Wouldn't the FBI launch an investigation? Wouldn't people be moving out of that neighborhood? My friend Jan wants to read your story too but I am mad at her so I didn't give it to her. You can give it to her if you still like her. I hope you will keep writing stories because I love reading them. Your friend, Ann.

CHAPTER 18: BIOLUMINESCENCE

In the morning, Cook discovered Ronald was not in his room. She told Mrs. Matthews, who was still in her nightgown, drinking a cup of coffee.

"What do you mean, he's not in his room? Of course, he is!"

The two women searched the house until Mrs. Matthews discovered the back door was cracked open. She yelled at Cook—as if it was Cook's fault.

Ronald was lying in the back yard unconscious, with a smile on his face. They thought he was dead, but he was only asleep. They shook him awake and got him up on his feet and back into the house, back into his room, and into his bed. Ronald was wearing protective clothing—his mother's.

"Fireflies are beautiful," Ronald said. Then he closed his eyes and went back to sleep.

When Ronald opened his eyes again, he was still in his bed. Cook was on one side of his bed. Mrs. Matthews was on the other side. They were wearing masks.

"I had the most wonderful dream," Ronald said.

"It weren't no dream," Cook said.

The night before, Ronald had awoken after midnight with a peculiar idea stuck in his mind. *If you want something bad enough, it just comes true.* He wanted to walk out of his room. He wanted to leave his house. He wanted to go outside. He told himself: *Anything is possible if you believe it hard enough.*

The door to his room was sealed, but it was not locked. He opened it. The air from the other side of the door did not seem any different than the air inside his room. He took a step into the next room. He was barefoot. The floor was made of wood. He took a step and another step and another. Ordinarily, he could see that room but only from inside his bedroom. Now, he was in the middle of the room, and everything looked different, the chairs and the little table with its vase of flowers. Roses. He could smell them. He crossed the room. *I can do anything*, he told himself, *if only I believe hard enough.* He opened a door and looked into a dark bedroom. Cook was asleep in her bed, snoring slightly. He closed her door and went farther down a hallway and opened another door. His mother was asleep in her bed. She was beautiful. People asleep are more beautiful than when they are awake. He never knew this before. He opened his mother's closet and found her protective clothing. It was a wonderful thing. He and his mother were practically the same size.

Ronald got into the one-piece suit and zipped it up. He pulled on the protective booties. He put on the face mask and the gloves.

He opened the back door and left the house. The night sky was full of stars. There wasn't any moon. *I believe*, Ronald thought, *I believe I believe I believe.* And then, some of the stars began to move, dance, and finally he realized they were not stars, but fireflies. Hundreds of soft-bodied beetles filled the air with bioluminescence and transformed the back yard into a wonderland.

"I don't know what happened after that," Ronald told Cook and his mother.

Mrs. Matthews said, "You fainted, honey."

Cook said it was a pure miracle Ronald was still alive.

Mrs. Matthews said, "Please, please, PLEASE, promise me you will never do that again!"

CHAPTER 19: NOT VERY BRIGHT

The night after Ronald visited the back yard, he took a turn for the worse. His temperature shot up. He started coughing and couldn't stop. He developed hives on his throat and face and had trouble breathing. An ambulance came and got him.

When he was returned a week later to his room, a lock had been installed on its door. Ronald asked Cook why the lock was necessary, and Cook said, "Because somebody I know is not very bright."

Ronald thought about writing another story. It would be about a firefly. He read about them in Dr. Fabber's *Guide*. "Not Very Bright" would be the title of his story. It would be about a male firefly who took off every night and flashed for all he was worth, but no females flashed back, because his flash was too dim. Ronald discovered there is a variety of firefly known as the femme fatale. It stays on the ground and winks at males. When they land, expecting to find love, the femme fatale eats them.

He told Cook his idea. She said, "What is it with you and these horrifying endings? Did you ever hear of a happy ending? People like them."

One good thing was that the neighbor kids, Mary Margaret, Jan and Josh, Max and Ann, found out about his escape from his room. One afternoon, Ronald looked out his window and the five kids were standing out there in a line as if they had been waiting for him to appear in the window. He felt self-conscious because he was in his pajamas, but he managed to smile and wave at them. Each of the kids was holding a spiral notebook and a marker pen. They wrote words in big letters on a page of their spiral notebooks and then held them up so Ronald could read them.

HI! CAN YOU. COME OUT?

When Cook noticed the kids, she went outside and ran them off, telling them not to encourage Ronald because if he went out into the normal world again, he might die.

Ronald made hand-written copies of his already finished stories, gave them to Cook, and instructed her to deliver them to the neighbor kids.

"Tell them they do not have to be returned and can be shared with other kids. Tell them I'm hard at work on a new story."

But that was a lie.

Ronald wished he was hard at work on a new story, but in fact he was having trouble. He unfolded the letter full of questions that Ann had written him. He studied it. He folded it up and put it in a drawer of his desk. He lay on his bed and looked up at the plastic stars on his ceiling.

He wished he had never said the wizard had had his house sprayed with pesticides because how were the boy and Melody ever going to invade the house and save Melody's father, who was trapped inside a jar in the basement? Maybe Melody could survive a trip inside the wizard's house because she had that suit of invulnerability, but the boy was now a house fly. He was no longer poisonous, which meant he was vulnerable to practically everything, but especially to spiders. And what about that cat? In his last story, he had mentioned that the wizard owned a cat. Ronald wondered if cats chase flies. He would have to ask Cook. She would probably know.

What about all the missing people? He had not thought that through, just said that the wizard shrank lots of people. He had failed to consider all the ramifications. Ann was right. If half the people in the neighborhood had vanished, there would be a big reaction. Their relatives would go insane with worry. Police officers would be going from door to door, questioning everyone. The FBI would get involved.

He wished he had never said the wizard shrank so many people. But how else was he going to explain why the insects could talk? It was all Cook's fault. She was the one who first suggested the whole idea of talking insects. He wished his father had never sent him that big fat guidebook about insects and spiders.

Maybe he could say the wizard cast a spell over the entire neighborhood, a magic spell that caused everyone to experience amnesia. They didn't report their missing family members because they couldn't remember them.

Ronald had a peculiar but interesting thought. Maybe the magic amnesia that affected everyone in the neighborhood was wearing off because the wizard no longer had his magic ring. He could say magic amnesia has to be renewed every few months, or else people start remembering their missing relatives. That might be cool.

He imagined a housewife finding a box of cigars in her bedroom and wondering who it belonged to because she didn't smoke. Her kids didn't smoke. And then, suddenly, she remembered, "Oh, my goodness, I had a husband! He smoked cigars, and his name was Tony!"

All over the neighborhood, adults would start remembering they used to have more kids.

Husbands would remember they used to have a wife. Kids would remember they used to have TWO parents, not just one.

"Where is everyone?!"

Of course, suspicion would soon turn to the wizard, that weird bald man who was always crawling around in his back yard with a magnifying glass.

Ronald looked up at the plastic stars and sighed. Writing stories was just too difficult.

When Ronald finished his new story, Cook put it in a manila envelope. On the outside of the envelope, she wrote NEW STORY. She taped the envelope to the front door. That evening, she told Ronald, "One of them kids must have come and got it, because it's gone. I hope you're happy."

Ronald attempted to smile but in fact he was not happy. He was nervous. Maybe the neighbor kids would hate his story.

THE CAT,
a new story by Ronald Matthews

The bearded man was in his jar with pretty much nothing to do. He had been stuck in the jar for weeks. He thought about his daughter, his only child, and missed her. He hummed to himself, which was his habit. Some men trapped in a jar might talk to themselves. What this man did was hum. He probably didn't even know he was doing it. He had a beard, black with grey streaks. It kept getting longer and scragglier because he had no way to trim it. He sat cross-legged on the bottom of the jar and stroked his long beard with his fingers and hummed.

What did he eat? How did the man survive in that jar?

There were holes in the top of the jar. It had one of those screw top lids. The lid had holes in it so he could breathe. The glass walls of the jar were so slippery, he couldn't climb up the sides and escape, so the jar was a pretty effective prison.

What did he eat?

Once a day, the evil wizard came and unscrewed the lid of the jar. When he did this, he picked up the jar, knocking the bearded man off his feet and throwing him from one side of the jar to the other. Then the wizard set the jar back down—it was sitting on top of an old wooden bench in his basement. The wizard tapped a little fish food into the jar, and then he closed the screw lid.

That was all the bearded man ever got to eat, fish food.

Fish food is a combination of squid meal, shrimp meal, earthworms, vitamins, and minerals. It's not that nasty to eat once you get used to it, but, unless you are a fish, it gets monotonous.

One night, the bearded man had trouble sleeping. He sat cross-legged on the bottom of the jar, gnawing on a bit of dried earthworm. He hummed to himself, thinking of his daughter, Melody. He figured Melody must miss him and wondered who was taking care of her. Melody was pretty resourceful, but she was only 13 years old. He wished he had told her what he was going to do. He'd left her a note saying he would be gone two weeks but did not tell her what exactly he was going to do because it sounded so crazy. He had made a deal with the wizard. He now thought he was stupid and reckless to do that. Only a fool would make a deal with a wizard.

The bearded man was an entomologist. An entomologist is a person who studies insects and spiders. He wanted to be the very best entomologist in the whole world. The deal he made with the wizard was that the wizard would shrink him until he was no taller than a cricket, provide him a suit of invulnerability, and turn him loose in the wizard's back yard, where he would research the lives of insects and spiders. After the two weeks were up, the wizard would make him normal sized again. His little notebook would be full of wonderful new information about the behavior of insects and spiders. It had seemed a perfect plan. The wizard had not even charged him that much money.

Unfortunately, the wizard had never fulfilled his end of the bargain. He had indeed shrunk the bearded man until he was smaller than a cricket, but he never provided him with a suit of invulnerability, and instead of putting him in the back yard where he could study insects and spiders, he had dropped him into a jar and put the jar on a wooden bench down in his basement.

The bearded man had been there ever since. How long? He had lost track of time. The wizard's basement did not have any windows. It would have been completely dark except that there was a light turned on, a dim light, halfway across the basement. If that lightbulb ever burned out, the bearded man would be plunged into total darkness.

Sometimes, the bearded man was visited by a centipede. Centipedes do not have eyes, but they have an excellent sense of smell. This particular centipede would have been happy to eat the bearded man, who smelled like delicious fish food, but it had no way to get into the jar. The centipede and the bearded man sometimes had conversations. The bearded man liked to ask the centipede, "Hey there, if you ever meet up with a girl named Melody, could you let her know her father is trapped in a jar in the wizard's basement and would appreciate it if she'd come and save him?" The centipede said he would of course do this. But the promise seemed silly because how likely was it that the centipede would ever meet up with the girl?

Occasionally, the bearded man in the jar was visited by a cat. When the cat was in the basement, the centipede never came to visit the bearded man in the jar because cats like to play with centipedes. They toy with them until they get bored, and then they eat the centipedes. To keep himself safe, the centipede hid in the basement walls until the cat went back upstairs.

The cat had heard the bearded man humming. Cats have excellent hearing. Its ears twitched as it listened to the tune coming from far away, from the basement. The cat stretched and walked to the basement door, which was open just a crack. The cat shouldered the door all the way open and ran down the steps into the dark basement. There was not much light down there but more than enough for the cat. Cats have excellent eyesight.

The humming was coming from a jar that was sitting on top of a wooden bench. The cat leapt up on the bench and peered into the jar. A bearded man was in there, a tiny human being, no bigger than a cricket. The cat licked its jaws. It reached out with one of its front paws and gave the jar a little shove.

The End.

(If you guys want another story, let me know. Your friend, Ronald.)

CHAPTER 20: I THINK I LOVE YOU

Hey, think about this, buddy. The guy in the jar has to poop and pee so there would be a lot of that in his jar probably a couple inches deep that would be cool. Get it? The whole jar would stink. Instead of hearing the humming, the cat could smell it and go down there to investigate. Just an idea hope you like it. MAX

Dear Ronald, I liked your story, especially the cat. My cat Fluffy is always pushing stuff off shelves so I thought it was cool when the wizard's cat did that. I liked the new story but want to know more about the girl with black and white hair. The stories about her are my favorites. I hope she finds her dad. I hate the evil wizard. Also, I hate centipedes, I hate hate hate them! I don't understand how the bearded man would even know Melody is insect-size now. You need to explain that. We're back in school. Jan and me and Mary Margaret are in seventh grade. Max and Josh in eighth. I hate gym class, but algebra is worse. You're so lucky you don't have to take algebra. My favorite class is art. When I get bored, I draw pictures of horses. I love horses so much. There's this girl Jessica I know she has her own horse, but we are not really friends. I love the Jackson 5 and David Cassidy. My mom's favorite show is Dr Welby which is about a doctor. My favorite is the Partridge Family because it has David Cassidy in it. I Think I Love You is my favorite song. I don't get to see

Ann's letter concluded with a row of numbers and a drawing of a horse.

Ronald asked Cook what all the numbers meant.

"What numbers?"

"These numbers." Ronald was on his side of the door and Cook was on her side. They were using the telephone to communicate. Ronald pressed the letter up against the window, so Cook could read it.

"What does Jackson 5 mean and who's David Cassidy?"

"Hold your horses," Cook put on her glasses, "give me a second." When Cook finished reading the letter, she took off her glasses.

"*The Partridge Family* is a TV show. You know what that is. David Cassidy must be a singer. That's my best guess. Who knows what Jackson 5 is? Probably another show."

For Ronald, TV was a painful memory. His mother had wheeled a TV set into his room a year ago and turned it on for him, but he was soon overwhelmed by the rapidly changing images and music and talking and noise. He couldn't figure it out and got sick to his stomach and had to lay down. He much preferred books. He had asked his mom to take away the TV.

Cook said, "The numbers are her phone number. She wants you to call her."

"Call her what?"

Cook rolled her eyes. Sometimes Ronald was so ignorant, it was just amazing. He read books all the time and he had a big vocabulary, so you could imagine he was smart, and then something like this would happen, and you would realize he was ignorant about even the simplest things. She explained that his telephone could be used to call people. She explained what a telephone number is and how to use the rotary dial on his phone.

Ronald was shocked. It had never occurred to him that something like that was possible. You could just dial a number, and somewhere else in the world, a person would pick up a telephone, and you could talk to that person even if you were a hundred miles away. Possibly he had read about this sort of thing at some point in his life, but even if he had, it had never dawned on him that this phone here in his room could be used for that purpose. When Cook or Ronald's mother wanted to use the phone to talk to him, they just rapped on the window. When he looked up from whatever he was doing—usually reading a book; he was now reading *Twenty Thousand Leagues Under the Sea* by Jules Verne—they would hold up the phone on their side. He would come to the window and pick up the phone attached to the wall on his side. Then they would talk. There was no need for any ringing.

According to Cook, Ronald's phone could ring. Someone—anyone, including Ann—could call him. Or he could call Ann.

Ronald thought about calling the number that would connect him to Ann, but he got nervous. What would he say to her when she answered the phone? He doubted she was reading *Twenty Thousand Leagues Under the Sea*.

He read the sentence in Ann's letter that included the words, "I think I love you." That was his favorite sentence in the letter even though Cook had explained that Ann did not mean she loved Ronald. She meant she loved a song titled "I Think I Love You." Cook said kids are always listening to rock and roll songs on the radio or on their record players. "I Think I Love You" must be one of those songs. Cook told him she was sure his mom would buy him a record player, and then he could listen to Ann's favorite song.

Two days later, Ronald owned a record player and *The Partridge Family* album. "I Think I Love You" was the fourth song on Side 2. Ronald learned how to drop the needle into the groove. He listened to "I Think I Love You" over and over until he knew all the words and could sing along.

Cook told Mrs. Matthews she thought Ronald was losing his mind.

"I hear him in there singing that stupid song. But will he call up that girl? He's scared to do it."

"Which one is it? The blonde or the chubby one?"

"The chubby one. With the dark hair."

Mrs. Matthews made a sound that could have been a laugh or possibly a snort.

Cook said, "I could give the girl his phone number."

Ronald had a watch, a present from his mother which was strapped to his wrist. He had never had much use for it but liked wearing it. Now he had a use for it. Cook told him Ann and the other kids were in school from nine to four every day. When the little hand and the big hand were in the right places, Ronald liked to imagine he was at school with them, maybe in algebra class, or in art class.

Cook had given Ronald instructions on how to use the phone.

"Dial the numbers. Press the receiver to your ear and listen to the rings. Someone will answer and say, 'Hello?' Then you say, 'Hi, this is Ronald Matthews, may I speak to Ann please?' If they say she isn't there, you say, 'Please, may I leave a message? Tell her Ronald Matthews called.' Then you say thank you and hang up."

Unfortunately, every time Ronald attempted to follow the instructions and call Ann, he lost his nerve. Finally, Cook couldn't stand it anymore. She gave the neighbor girl Ronald's phone number.

That evening, Ronald was shocked out of his thoughts by the ringing of the telephone in his room. He laid down the book he was reading, *Oliver Twist*, by Charles Dickens, and picked up the phone, an action which caused it to stop ringing. He pressed the receiver against his ear and said in a very loud voice,

"HELLO, THIS IS RONALD MATTHEWS!"

"Geez, you don't have to shout. It's me, Ann."

"THIS IS RONALD MATTHEWS! WHO IS THIS?"

"You have a really loud voice! It's Ann."

Fifteen minutes later, Ronald's thoughts were in a swirl. His face was hot, his hands were sweaty, and he could hardly remember the phone conversation he had just concluded. Fortunately, Ann had done most of the talking. She had told him a lot of stuff about David Cassidy and her favorite show *The Partridge Family*. She had told him she was now friends with the girl named Jessica who owned a horse named Sugar, and how she hoped to get to ride on Sugar and brush out her mane and tail. She had said she liked his stories even if they didn't always make sense and wanted to know what happened after the cat pushed the jar containing Melody's dad off the bench.

When Ronald hung up the phone, he was very happy. His heart was beating fast, too fast. He had to lie down on his bed and look up at the plastic stars on his ceiling.

CHAPTER 21: YOU CAN'T JUST LEAVE PEOPLE HANGING

Ronald was reading another Dickens novel, *A Tale of Two Cities*. At least he was attempting to read it. Unfortunately, he was having trouble concentrating. In the novel, cruel aristocrats were getting their heads chopped off. The novel included angry mobs, guillotines, and a creepy old woman who knitted down the names of her victims, the aristocrats. You would think something like that would hold Ronald's attention, but in fact he was thinking about his telephone. The characters in the novel did not have stuff like telephones and record players. He wanted to lay down his book and pick up the telephone receiver. He wanted to dial Ann's number. All he had to do was go over there by the door where the phone was attached to the wall and do it. What could be easier? He read a paragraph of *A Tale of Two Cities*. He had read this same paragraph four times already but could never remember what it was about. Ronald told himself that he was a coward, a miserable stupid coward. Maybe if he thought about Ann, if he repeated the phrase *Call Me* in his mind, SHE would suddenly have the desire to call HIM.

Ronald thought: *Call me call me call me.*

His phone did not ring.

Call me call me call me call me!

It was Saturday afternoon and fall sunlight was streaming into his window. Yellow and orange leaves from the big tree in the field beyond his window were drifting to the ground. A breeze was blowing them in the general direction of his house. No one was out there. No boys or girls. Probably there were millions of insects out there. You couldn't see them, but they were in the grass. Grasshoppers. Crickets. Ants.

It was early October. At night, the air temperature outside got so cool that all the insects slowed down, stopped, froze in place like statues. When the sun came up, their cold-blooded bodies started to warm up. Their antennae twitched; a leg moved. They returned to life.

Insects never did anything stupid like wait for a phone to ring. Ants and grasshoppers and crickets are not miserable cowards.

Ronald dialed Ann's number. The phone rang three times. A man's voice answered. Probably Ann's father. The deep voice scared Ronald and he hung up.

Ronald hit himself in the head. He hit his forehead with the heels of his hands. He did this several times until there were red marks on his forehead. Why was he so stupid?

Stupid, stupid, stupid!

An hour later, Ronald tried again. This time he got another deep voice, a different one. Probably Ann's older brother, Max. "Yeah?"

"Is Ann there?" Ronald said.

"Hey, Fatso! It's for you. It's a BOY!"

A moment later, Ronald was talking to Ann. It was amazing.

Ann advised Ronald not to call her friend Mary Margaret because Mary Margaret now had a boyfriend named Eric who would not like her talking on the phone to another boy, even a very sick boy like Ronald. Eric was a hothead. If he heard Mary Margaret was talking to Ronald, he'd probably show up outside Ronald's window and yell at him. He might even throw a rock through his window.

"And that might kill you, right? All that dust and pollen and poisons pouring into your room!"

Ronald explained that his window was multilayered, unbreakable, and bulletproof, so probably the worst thing that would happen, the rock would just bounce off, but he promised to take Ann's advice and not call Mary Margaret. He didn't know her number anyway.

A week later, Ann called Ronald and told him she had big news. Ann's horse-owning friend Jessica was now Eric's new girlfriend. Mary Margaret was heartbroken. She didn't even want to go to school anymore. But the good side of it was that Mary Margaret and Ann were friends again.

Ann and Ronald were now talking on the phone nearly every day. Ronald learned a great deal about the TV show *The Partridge Family*. New episodes ran on Friday nights. Every Saturday morning, after she ate breakfast, Ann called Ronald to tell him the plot of the latest episode. The Partridge Family owned a bus. Every week, they went somewhere really cool like Las Vegas and played rock and roll songs. They were super popular. David Cassidy was the lead singer. He was probably the coolest boy in the entire universe. In the show, David had a sister named Laurie played by the actress Susan Dey. If Ann could have just one wish she would want to look exactly like Susan Dey, because Susan Dey had the perfect slim body and the perfect blue eyes and the perfect smile and the perfect brown hair. Everything about Susan Dey was perfection. Ann wished that her family could buy a bus and go on the road playing rock and roll songs for adoring audiences, but no one in her family had any musical talent.

The one talent that Ann did have was art. She loved to draw pictures.

Mrs. Matthews, Ronald's mother, did not entirely approve of Ronald's phone calls to Ann. She had mixed feelings. She felt it was a good thing that Ronald had a friend, a phone pal. But she had noticed he was no longer writing stories about the Insect Boy, and he seemed less and less interested in reading books. Ronald often seemed restless, moody, unsatisfied with his life. Talking to Ann was making him want to be different, but how much could he change? Ronald was delicate and fragile. She was worried he might try again to escape his room, explore the outer world, and if he did, who knew what might happen?

Sometimes, when Ronald called Ann's house, Max answered the phone and insisted on talking to Ronald. He had ideas. Max thought Ronald should get his sister Ann to draw pictures of Insect Boy. He thought that would be really cool.

"I'm telling you, people like books with illustrations. For example, Ann should draw a picture of Insect Boy looking scared and a giant praying mantis looking down at him because it wanted to eat him. That would be scary cool. She'd do it if you ask her. Why don't you ask her? All she does now is draw stupid pictures of horses and stupid David Cassidy."

Max had read Ronald's last story, the one about the bearded man, and he wanted to know what happened next. What happened after the cat pushed the jar containing the bearded man off the shelf? Did the bearded guy get smashed to death?

Did the cat jump down and catch the bearded guy and play with him the way cats play with mice?

"It's horrible what cats do to mice!" Max said. "You can't just write stories like that and leave people hanging!"

Max wanted more violence, more fighting. He said Ronald's hero was too soft and wussy. He said he had a good idea for the ending.

"The girl, Melody, with her power over grasshoppers, kills the wizard with an invading army of hoppers. That would be so cool. The wizard disappears beneath thousands of hoppers and is eaten alive, nothing left but his skeleton. That would be so badass!"

The real reason Ronald did not write another story was because he was overwhelmed by the multiplying questions.

Why did the wizard shrink all these people?

Why did the magic ring work for Melody at first but now it doesn't?

Why did the boy turn into a common housefly but not completely, not his head?

What happened after the cat pushed Dr. Fabber's jar off the shelf?

THE ANSWERS TO ALL THE QUESTIONS, a new
story by Ronald Matthews

Why does the evil wizard do so many bad things? Why does he shrink people and turn them into insects? Because he's evil; that's why. He's a lonely loser and has no friends, so he hates everyone who has a family, everyone normal. Also, he has a nose that looks like a potato. He has ulcers and migraine headaches and diarrhea and asthma. He's not a happy person. If he meets anyone happy, he hates that person.

What about that ring? Why doesn't the ring work anymore? It's supposed to be magic, right? You want to know the dark and magical reason the ring does not work for Melody? It, the ring, hates her!

The ring is alive. Long ago, another wizard, a bad one, was captured and punished by a good wizard. The good wizard turned the evil one into a ring and put him in a desk drawer and forgot about him. The evil wizard, now a ring, lay in the darkness of the drawer for a thousand years. The ring gradually forgot all about being a wizard. All it recalled was that it enjoyed being evil. And then one day, the drawer was opened. After a long quest, the evil wizard, the modern one, discovered the ancient desk, opened its secret drawer, and picked up the ring. The Magic Ring That Loved Evil!

The wizard put the ring on his third finger. For a moment he felt dizzy, as if he was going to faint. Then he felt as if he was going to vomit. Black spots swam before his eyes. His entire body felt hot and tingly. He felt taller. Uglier. More evil!

He now possessed the Power of the Ring! He was the most powerful wizard in the history of wizardry! Think of all the evil he could do! He could rule the world! He could turn all the good people, the nice ones who had friends and families into his slaves. One by one, he would turn them into insects and force them to carry out his evil commands. He was creating an army! An army of insects!

Unfortunately, the ring was too small for his finger. It pinched. In fact, it is not possible to wear a ring like that, full of evil magic, and not experience at least a little pain. At night, when he went to bed, the evil wizard took off the ring, lay it on the little table by his bed, and rubbed his sore finger until the pain went away. Then he went to sleep.

One morning, when he woke up, the ring was gone! It had been stolen!

I know what you are thinking. How did the wizard figure out that Melody had his ring? How did he learn she was the one who had stolen his Suit of Invulnerability and his sword? How did he know Melody had used the magic ring to shrink herself and was wandering around in his back yard looking for her father, Dr. Fabber, the famous entomologist, who was trapped in a jar in his basement?

The ring told him! It had a dark and magical way of communicating with the wizard. When the evil wizard was asleep—he was getting old and he was fond of naps—the ring entered his dreams, begged the evil wizard to come save him. *Master, I have been captured by a horribly good girl. I hate her. Help! Come save me! I am on her hand. On her thumb.*

The ring was so upset about being on Melody's thumb that every day it made itself a little bit smaller so that it could hurt the girl by pinching her thumb. No matter what she said to the ring, no matter how much Melody wanted to use it to do magic, the ring would not assist her. It did not like her. It hated anyone who was good.

Please, Master, find me, the ring whispered to the sleeping wizard. *Save me.*

OK. Where did we leave off?

Oh, yeah, we were in the wizard's basement. Dr. Fabber was trapped in a jar, and the wizard's cat had pushed the jar off the bench.

Luckily, Dr. Fabber did not break any bones. He was flung under an old sofa. The cat jumped down from the bench, tiptoed through the broken glass, and attempted to reach under the sofa with her paw and capture Dr. Fabber, but he stayed out of reach.

Dr. Fabber hid under the sofa for a long time waiting for the cat to get bored and go away and for his head to quit spinning. It is pretty depressing to be stuck in a jar with nothing to eat but fish food for weeks, and then the next thing you know a monstrous cat knocks your jar over, and it's as if you are in the middle of a huge explosion. You are flung under a sofa, lucky to be alive. Your ears are ringing, and before you can even gather your wits, the giant paw of the monster cat is trying to grab you with its extended claws. Dr. Fabber crawled backwards and got as far away from that paw as he could.

Eventually, he escaped the house. Don't ask me how. I can't know everything. He was darn lucky he did not die because there were puddles of insecticide all over that basement. How did Dr. Fabber avoid dying of insecticide? He pinched his nose and held his breath whenever the stink got too bad. He tiptoed around the puddles of poison.

Hours later, Dr. Fabber found himself outdoors. He had escaped from the wizard's basement. Somehow, miraculously, Dr. Fabber was free! He was exactly where he had always wanted to be, in the grass forest, in the world of insects.

That is when he realized he was being observed.

CHAPTER 22: PRAISE, NOT SUGGESTIONS

Cook and Mrs. Matthews looked at Ronald. They were on the other side of the door to Ronald's room, looking through the window. It was only 9 PM and Ronald was already asleep in his bed.

Cook said she thought Ronald was experiencing another growth spurt.

"That's why he's sleeping so much."

Mrs. Matthews said, "He's so moody!"

Cook shrugged.

Mrs. Matthews said, "Did he like that record album I bought him? It was a classical sampler full of music by Mozart and Hayden. I want him to like, you know, GOOD music."

"He listened to it and fell asleep."

"If you ask me, those neighbor kids have too much influence on him. What are their names? The pudgy ones."

"Max is the boy and Ann is the girl. '

"He needs better friends."

Cook grunted.

"Is he doing his exercises? The doctors say he needs to exercise."

"Now, it's mostly just the pacing."

"Pacing!"

"He paces back and forth in there, like a lion in a cage. For up to 45 minutes at a time. And talks to himself while he's doing it. And when he ain't pacing, he's dancing."

"Dancing?!"

"He wants a curtain for this window. He says he needs more privacy."

"That is simply impossible. His health is too delicate. We need to monitor him. I hope you told him that."

"What can you do? He's a teenage boy."

Mrs. Matthews and Cook remembered what they got up to when they were teenagers. They looked at Ronald trapped in his hermetically sealed room and sighed, feeling sorry for him.

Cook said, "He wants a Jackson 5 record 'ABC it's easy as 1, 2, 3,' and this book—what is it called? —I wrote it down, *Lord of the Rings*."

"I'll put it on the list. How does he even find out about these things?"

"Today he demanded a radio. And a Milwaukee Bucks jersey and a basketball."

"We don't even live in Milwaukee! We live in Chicago!"

"His buddy Max loves the Milwaukee Bucks, so now he does too."

"Is he still running a slight fever at night?"

"Sometimes."

"You're still listening in on his phone calls, I hope."

Cook shrugged.

"Is he still writing those horrible stories about insects?"

"It's his hobby."

The two women who loved him looked through the window at Ronald. Mrs. Matthews said, "He was so beautiful when he was four years old. Remember?"

On the phone, Ann told Ronald, "Max and I read your story. You need a better title than The Answers to All the Questions by Ronald Matthews. Use your imagination! We think it's cool that the ring is alive and wants to return to its master, but that same idea is used in *The Lord of the Rings*. You want everyone in the world to think you're just copying? It's still a cool idea even if you are copying. The dream connection between the ring and the wizard is totally cool. Me and Jan don't completely understand it, but it's cool. We're still wondering why the boy has his human head. You need to explain that. We love that the story ends with someone observing him, but we hope it's not another spider because you've already got too many chapters with spiders in them. The whole tone of the last story is grumpy. Like you're mad at your readers. We're just trying to be helpful. I'm going to draw a picture of the boy looking up at a praying mantis. A scary one! Even though praying mantises are super hard to draw. You can put it on the cover!"

The rest of the conversation—it was more like a monologue than a conversation because Ann did all the talking—was about music. Ann said now that Ronald had a record player, he needed to buy more records.

"Especially 'They Long to Be Close to You' by the Carpenters. Oh my, it's so good! And 'Julie Do Ya Love Me' by Bobby Sherman who I adore almost as much as David Cassidy. I love him to pieces!"

After he hung up, Ronald examined his feelings and asked himself did he still want to share his stories with Ann and Max? What he really wanted from Max and Ann was praise, not suggestions. Not criticism! He thought about the dig about *The Lord of the Rings*. Ronald had never even heard of the book until Max went on and on about it, and he still hadn't read it. Accusing him of stealing his idea about the ring from it was most unfair.

He was now reading a book called *Journey to the Center of the Earth* by Jules Verne, another present from his father. Ronald thought it must be one of the greatest books ever written, all about a geology professor and his nephew Axel. It turned out, in the center of the earth, there was an entire subterranean world inhabited by prehistoric monsters! It was hard to believe *Lord of the Rings* could be even half as good as *Journey to the Center of the Earth.*

When his mother gave him a basketball, Ronald discovered it helped him relax when he dribbled it. Unfortunately, when he started bouncing it off the walls, he broke a lamp.

THE MONARCH,
a story by Ronald Matthews

After his escape from the wizard's basement, Dr. Fabber was gripped by nausea. He dropped to his hands and knees and vomited.

A monarch butterfly, perched on a nearby milkweed, watched him. This was no ordinary monarch. It had a human head, a pair of human arms held up by the chest, and a human chest and stomach. Attached to the human body were four insect legs which the monarch used for walking and for perching as it was doing now. "Are you alright?" it asked. "You don't look well."

Dr. Fabber vomited again.

The monarch told Dr. Fabber it was obvious he had just come out of the wizard's house.

"Most insects who enter that house never come out alive. The reason you're sick is because the wizard's house is full of poison. Does the inside of your nose burn? Are your eyes watering? You're lucky to be alive."

Dr. Fabber wiped his sweaty face. He felt horrible. He sneezed loudly.

"You reek of poison," the monarch said. "Which is good in a way. Keeps the predators away. But if I were you, I would try milkweed. It's healthy and nutritious. I love it!" The monarch tore off a bit of a nearby leaf and chewed on it. "Even if you can't bring yourself to dine on milkweed leaves, maybe you can just rub yourself all over with milkweed milk? Take my word for it. That'll keep the predators away!"

Dr. Fabber sneezed four times in a row. Dr. Fabber was an expert on insects and did not need to be told that most predators avoid monarchs because they dine on milkweed, which is distasteful to predators. It gives the butterflies a weird smell.

"The sneezing, that's your nose trying to get rid of the insecticide. You must have breathed in the fumes. Nasty stuff." The monarch finished eating the bit of milkweed leaf and tore off another piece. "You're Dr. Fabber, I bet."

Dr. Fabber got to his feet. He still felt a bit wobbly.

"How do you know my name?"

Dr. Fabber knew that the wizard shrank people until they were as small as insects. In fact, he had paid the wizard to shrink him because he wanted to be the first entomologist in the history of entomology to study insects up close and personal, on their own level. He had heard the rumor that the people the wizard shrunk eventually turned into insects, but he had never believed it. However, Dr. Fabber was a scientist, trained to observe and to accept the evidence of his senses. Here was a monarch butterfly with a human body. He would need many more examples to be sure, but it did seem possible that the rumors were true. He felt a pang of regret because he had hoped to study ordinary insects, not insects who were partially human.

"I asked you a question. How do you know my name?"

"There's a girl down here, looking for you."

That was how Dr. Fabber found out his daughter Melody was here in the grass forest. He was so shocked, he had to sit down on the ground and gather his wits.

"She's with that other one, the boy who turned into a fly."

"A boy who ... Oh my! Oh, dear me! Has she, has Melody ... *turned*?" Dr. Fabber was so shocked that he could hardly finish asking his question. "Has Melody transformed into some kind of insect?"

"Not yet," the monarch said.

The monarch explained the whole deal to Dr. Fabber. When the wizard shrank people and left them in the grass forest, they soon began to forget about their earlier lives, when they were big. The more they forgot, the sooner they transformed into insects. Some victims clung to the memories of their former lives.

They found it impossible to forget their families, their friends, their jobs. People of that sort transformed much more slowly than the ones who forgot quickly. Dr. Fabber's daughter was fixated on finding him. Very likely that was why she had not transformed at all. The monarch explained that he too was still partially human. "It's because I miss my little dog, Mopsy. I've completely forgotten my wife, what's-her-name, but I miss Mopsy so much! And of course, accountancy."

"Accountancy?"

The monarch explained that he had been a tax accountant. He loved accounting.

"Numbers are so exciting! From the time I was a child I loved arithmetic!" He figured he still had most of his human body because he missed his little dog too. "We used to go for walks. Twice a day. Such a good boy! And coffee! Every morning I drank three cups of delicious black coffee! Maxwell House, good to the last drop! I miss it." The monarch said he had begun to forget other things. He was having trouble recalling what exactly a tax deduction was. "And loopholes. And apples."

"You can't recall what apples are?"

"I can't remember the difference between tomatoes and apples. Both are round red things, am I right? But how are they different? I can't recall. And what exactly is an armchair? Is it a chair made out of arms? And for that matter, what is a chair?"

"You don't remember what a chair is?!"

"Do you like my wings?" The former tax accountant spread his huge, gorgeous, orange and black wings.

"I have to find her!" Dr. Fabber said. "I have to get out of here! Before I change! Before Melody transforms! Where is she? Please tell me."

"When I completely forget my human life, I will very likely feel the need to fly to Mexico. But I don't need to tell you that. If you are indeed the famous Dr. Fabber, you must know all about monarchs and our annual migration down to Mexico."

"I do know about the migration of you monarchs. It's a wonderful thing. But please, my daughter, the girl you mentioned. Where is she? I must find her! I have to save her!"

"No idea," the monarch said. "But to be frank, there's no way to save her. No way to save any of us. Not as long as the wizard has his magic ring."

"His what?"

"Goodbye, Dr. Fabber. Good luck!" The monarch leapt up into a breeze and floated away like a sailing ship setting out on an ocean voyage. "Mexico, here I come!"

CHAPTER 23: HURRICANE IRENE

Ronald's mother, Mrs. Matthews, was afraid of almost no one. She was not afraid of her clients, the accused criminals, or judges or police officers, nor anyone else she normally met. She was, however, afraid of her Aunt Irene.

Aunt Irene was a formidable woman. That is the word Ronald's mother used to describe her, formidable. Others in the family called her an interfering old bat, but never to her face.

Aunt Irene was a white-haired, blue-eyed woman who always wore flat heels and blue suits. She walked rapidly. She had a loud ringing voice. She tended to look people in the eye. She loved to ask difficult and embarrassing questions. Many people in the Matthews family felt that, if they had a character defect, Aunt Irene would locate it. It was as if she possessed a superpower. She would locate their flaw, describe it in horrifying detail, and demand they eliminate it.

Once every few years, Aunt Irene went on an inspection tour of the entire Matthews family. A nephew or niece would receive a letter announcing her imminent arrival. On the appointed date, Aunt Irene would enter their house and begin her inspection. She would ask questions, expose secrets, find fault, suggest improvements, and then leave—on her way to improve another member of the family. No one in the family enjoyed or asked for these visits, but everyone believed that Aunt Irene, like the judgement of God, could not be escaped.

On Monday, the first day that Aunt Irene spent at Ronald's house, she interrogated Cook.

Somehow, without meaning to, Cook told her things. It was as if secrets Cook had never intended to reveal simply drifted out of her mouth.

After talking to Aunt Irene, Cook felt that she was too lazy and timid, too easy-going. Probably she should be fired. How had this happened? Why had she revealed so much? Cook had no idea.

On Tuesday, Aunt Irene interviewed Ronald's doctors. Although they were well trained physicians, they wound up feeling that perhaps they should give up medicine and take up careers as sanitation workers.

Wednesday afternoon, when Ronald's friends, Max and Ann, returned home from school, they found Aunt Irene sipping tea in their living room, talking to their mother.

Thursday morning, Aunt Irene read Ronald's stories about Insect Boy, all of them. That afternoon, Aunt Irene knocked on the window to Ronald's room. When he looked to see who it was, she held up the phone on her side of the window and indicated he should pick up the receiver on his side.

Several hours later, Ronald was lying on his bed with his eyes open, looking up at the plastic stars on his ceiling.

That night, Aunt Irene had a meeting with Ronald's mother and delivered her report.

The next morning, Aunt Irene departed, on her way to improve the next member of the family, a college professor who lived in Boston.

That evening, Mrs. Matthews sat in her kitchen, sipping a large glass of wine. She felt she was an atrocious, neglectful parent who loved her accused criminals more than she loved her own son. She felt that perhaps she should give up the practice of law and retire to a mental asylum.

THE REPORT ON RONALD MATTHEWS

Appearance? Ronald often spends his entire day in pajamas or else wears a tee shirt and shorts. He needs a haircut. Shoes and socks. He needs to work on his personal hygiene and posture. Ronald chews his fingernails. He often becomes shifty-eyed and drops his voice until he is barely audible. He does not exercise regularly. He is puny, pasty, and possesses soft undeveloped muscles. Surprisingly, except for the fact he is allergic to nearly everything, Ronald seems in good health.

Education? Ronald is unschooled and untutored. He reads whatever he likes. He rises when he feels like it and goes to bed when he feels like it. He possesses a record player and a radio and has become addicted to mushy love songs. He knows little about history except what he has learned by reading the fictional works of Charles Dickens and Jules Verne. Ronald knows no math beyond arithmetic. He thinks there is something called algebra but doesn't know what it is. He knows nothing about politics or government. When asked to identify the current president of the United States, he said, "It isn't Abe Lincoln, is it?" He knows very little about geography. When asked to locate Chicago, the city he lives in, on a world map, he pointed at the continent of Australia. He does not know his zip code or his street address. He knows nothing about art history and could not identify Picasso or Rembrandt. He has no practical skills like woodworking or welding. He has never gone shopping, never entered a grocery store, and is not familiar with money or check books.

Social Skills? Ronald spends his day with Cook, an elderly woman who allows him to do as he pleases. He has a telephone and uses it to have long, rambling conversations about nothing of significance with two neighbor children, neither of whom is in any way distinguished intellectually.

Parenting? Ronald's father has not seen Ronald in more than a year. When I asked, "Do you know where your father is?" Ronald replied, "Is he still in Bolivia?" His mother (I am talking about you, Margaret!) adores him but she is a hardworking attorney with many clients and has little time for him.

Bright spots? Ronald reads and writes far above his grade level and knows a surprising amount about entomology. He is the author of several morbid fairytales involving talking insects and a wizard. The hero of these stories is a boy who is transforming into a common housefly. One does not have to be Sigmund Freud to guess that Ronald's stories reveal Ronald's view of himself and his world. He fears he is barely human and is trapped in a dangerous world where he is constantly in danger of death.

Recommendations: Ronald should read the most inspiring book ever written, *The Story of My Life* by Helen Keller. He needs to know that obstacles are to be overcome! You should hire a tutor for Ronald, one who will organize and supervise his studies, preferably a man because he needs more male role models. Ronald should do calisthenics every day to build up his muscles. Ronald should be made to wear proper clothing during the day, preferably trousers and polo shirts.

He must wear shoes! His phone calls to his friends should be limited in duration.

CHAPTER 24: ANDY

Ronald's mother placed an ad for a tutor in a Chicago newspaper.

While he was waiting for his mom to hire someone, Ronald read *The Story of My Life* by Helen Keller. He could see why his aunt wanted him to read it. Helen Keller was a deaf and blind girl. She was practically a wild animal until she received the assistance of a tutor named Annie Sullivan. Miss Sullivan taught Helen how to communicate using finger movements. She taught the disadvantaged girl everything imaginable, how to wear clothes and brush her teeth, how to eat using table utensils. Eventually, the girl could talk and read (Braille). By the time she was an adult, Helen Keller was the most famous deaf and blind person in the entire world. She wrote books and articles and toured the world, giving inspiring speeches everywhere she went.

That is what a tutor could do for you.

The tutor Ronald's mom hired was named Andy.

Andy was a graduate student in the history department of a nearby university (DePaul). He was working on a dissertation that had to do with Ulysses S. Grant. He had been working on it for four years and not making much progress. Andy was very happy to accept the generous offer of Mrs. Matthews to tutor her son.

Ronald liked Andy right away. Andy was not only a student of history; he was also a student of the martial arts. Andy said diet was very important. Andy said, before you even think about doing anything productive, you should start your day by consuming a bowl of bran flakes with milk and then eat an orange or a half of grapefruit.

Unfortunately, Ronald was allergic to milk. He was also allergic to citrus.

Andy said, "Bananas, buddy." Andy always called Ronald "buddy."

After that conversation, Ronald ate a banana every day for breakfast.

He decided he liked his new nickname and told Cook and his mother, "From now on, I want to be called Buddy. Don't call me Ronald anymore."

Ronald's mother frowned and Cook made a growling noise.

At first, Andy communicated with Ronald only over the telephone. He called Ronald from his apartment, so Ronald had no idea what Andy looked like. But one Saturday morning, Andy appeared in the yard outside Ronald's window and led him in a round of calisthenics. Andy also demonstrated some cool karate chops.

Andy was tall and skinny and 30 years old. He had long arms and long legs and wore glasses. Because he was starting to lose the hair on top of his head. He liked to wear a baseball cap. The Chicago White Sox. He said only losers liked the Chicago Cubs.

Andy told Ronald, "Your mom is hot!"—an observation which made Ronald nervous. He told Ronald, "Know what your problem is? You suffer from low self-esteem."

With Andy's help, Ronald studied algebra, American history, American presidents, American wars, Native Americans, and American geography (capital cities, major rivers, and chief exports). Andy said the other countries in the world also contain cities and rivers, but theirs are not nearly as important as the American ones.

"You are one lucky dude, buddy. You live in the greatest country in the whole wide world!"

When Ronald could not make head nor tails out of algebra, Andy told him algebra is not that important.

"All you really need is arithmetic."

Andy told him, "You gotta dream big and think positive. Life is all about personal growth. Say goodbye to negative thinking! You want to live your entire life in this little room?"

When Andy found out that Ronald liked *The Story of My Life* by Helen Keller, he recommended Ronald read other inspiring books. He suggested Ronald read a book about a boy who was born without hands who became a great artist, using only his toes to hold the paint brushes.

Ronald loved this book.

Ronald's mother got him an alarm clock so he could start following a regular schedule. Every morning, at 7 AM, when his alarm clock went off, Ronald jumped out of bed, turned off the alarm, did all his exercises, even the leg lifts, and then took a shower. After his shower, he put on his newly purchased school uniform: brown shoes and black socks, grey trousers, a long-sleeved shirt and tie, and a navy-blue blazer with an emblem on the pocket. The emblem was a bald eagle. Andy said eagles are the biggest and bravest of all the birds. He said, even though Ronald was not attending a real school, the uniform would make him feel normal and do wonders for his self-esteem.

Most days, within an hour of putting it on, Ronald removed the jacket and loosened the tie. By lunch time, the shoes were unlaced, and the shirt tail had escaped the trousers. Still, Ronald felt his self-esteem was improving, and Andy thought so too.

When Andy gave Ronald karate lessons, Andy stood outside in the yard. Andy and Ronald wore white karate pajamas. Andy's pajamas had a black belt. Ronald's had a white one. Even though it was almost Halloween, and it was starting to get chilly outdoors, Andy and Ronald were barefoot. Ronald felt bad about the situation because he was inside his room where it was warm and comfortable, but Andy had to be outside in the cold.

Andy said, "I'll tell you a secret, buddy. When I'm doing karate, I don't even feel the cold. I'm in the zone. It's all about focus. Know what I mean? Concentration! I transcend the cold!"

To the best of his ability, Ronald imitated the moves that Andy showed him. It felt more like dancing than fighting, and sometimes Ronald wished he could karate chop a real opponent.

According to Andy, Ronald should not worry about that sort of thing.

"Don't overthink it. Stay positive, little buddy. You're well on your way to earning that yellow belt!"

Andy told Ronald he was lucky he was learning karate and not judo or kung fu.

"Judo and kung fu are great in their way. I'm not gonna disrespect them. But they are forms of defensive fighting. Karate is way better because karate is aggressive. Know what I mean? With one good chop, you can shatter your enemy's forearm. With one well-placed kick, you can smash in two of his ribs."

Ronald wished he had an enemy because he would like to smash in a bad person's ribs—like a criminal or a rapist or someone like that. Ronald liked to imagine he was outside at night, just roaming around and not having any kind of allergy attack, and he saw someone, a beautiful girl being attacked by a mugger. The girl was screaming, and the mugger was laughing in that horrible way bad guys laugh. Using his karate chops and kicks, Ronald smashed the bad guy into little pieces.

The girl was very grateful.

Ronald soon came to believe that Andy was the greatest male role model in the whole world.

When he was not reading inspiring stories about courageous people who overcame their disabilities, or studying about the pioneers, or filling out worksheets about the presidents, or drawing a map of the Great Lakes, or doing his exercises, or working on his karate moves or talking on the phone to his friends Max and Ann, Ronald worked on the next chapter of his Insect Boy saga. At least he tried to. He wanted to write a new kind of story, the kind that Andy would like. His hero, the boy, should be braver and more resourceful. A real hero would get the better of the evil wizard, maybe even kill him. Unfortunately, each time Ronald tried to write that kind of story, it soon fell apart and he could not finish it. Sometimes Ronald suspected he was not in control of his stories; they were in control of him. Well, that was going to change. Think positive! Say bye-bye to negative thoughts! He did his exercises, and he practiced his favorite karate moves until he got into a wonderful mood. And then he started his new story.

THE HAPPY ENDING,
a story by Buddy Matthews

Without his magic ring, the wizard was just an average person. His spells began to evaporate. He had shrunk hundreds of people and then enchanted their relatives, so they did not even remember the missing people. Many of his victims down there in the grass forest of his back yard turned into insects. The boy, for example, was almost entirely a house fly. Only his head was still human. Without his magic ring, the wizard could not renew his spells. That was important, because spells need regular renewal, or else they will start to fade. All over the wizard's neighborhood, people began to remember their missing loved ones.

"I used to have a husband."

"Hey, know what? Pretty sure I used to have a mother."

"Didn't we used to have four kids, not just three? Where's Joanie?"

"Have you guys seen Grandma?"

Down in the grass forest, the wizard's victims began to change. They got itchy all over and, the next thing they knew, their insect legs turned back into human legs and human arms. It was wonderful! Even more amazing, they started to grow! They grew and grew until they were normal sized again!

All over the neighborhood, there were happy reunions.

"Daddy, where you been? We missed you so much!"

"Mommy!"

"Joanie!"

"Grandma!"

Pretty soon, a bunch of people marched to the police station and complained about the wizard. People had signs. ARREST THE WIZARD! MURDER THE MAGICIAN! The FBI got involved, and the state police, The Highway Patrol and the Coast Guard, the Army, the Navy, and even the CIA.

The wizard had broken ten thousand laws and had to be punished. *You can't just go around turning people into Insects!*

The wizard was arrested and led off to jail. After his trial, he was sent to prison, sentenced to one thousand life terms with no chance of parole. That was the end of his mischief.

The boy became a real boy again, normal-sized, with a human body. The girl, Melody, was reunited with her beloved father, the renowned entomologist, Dr. Henry Fabber.

She and the boy grew up, fell in love, and got married.

Everyone (except the wizard) lived happily ever after.

The End

Ronald made a copy of his new story, doing his best to make his handwriting legible, and gave it to Cook to read. Cook read it and sniffed, "If you ask me, it needs more salt."

Ronald thought this comment just showed how stupid Cook was. Clearly, she was a negative thinker.

Cook taped the new story to the front door, and Max and Ann came and got it.

The next day, Max and Ann reported that they did not like the new story. What about the various loose ends? For example, what about all the insects, former people who got eaten? How could they come back to their families when they were dead?

Ann said in her opinion the ending would be better if Insect Boy and Melody teamed up to bring down the wizard. When a boy and a girl team up to defeat evil, they fall in love. It's just natural. Then, and only then, at the end of the story, after their triumph, Insect Boy and Melody could get married. Or at least engaged.

Max said he hoped Ronald wouldn't let himself get carried away with the stupid love stuff. Too much love totally wrecks a story. Max said he still recommended that an army of grasshoppers led by the boy (assisted by the girl) should jump on top of the wizard and devour him.

"There should be, like, LOTS OF SCREAMING. Know what I mean? And blood and stuff. And then, *nothing left but bones*. That would be so badass."

Ronald felt that his friends were just as stupid as Cook. On the phone, he asked his tutor Andy, "Have you read my stories yet? I wrote a new one. I wrote a happy ending."

Andy said he'd tried to carve out a little time to read Ronald's stories.

"I want to, buddy. There's nothing I'd rather do than read a story written by a 14-year-old kid." Andy said, unfortunately, he had to read a million scholarly articles about Ulysses S. Grant because of his dissertation, so he didn't have time to read stories about bugs. He said he was pretty sure publishers weren't looking for stories about bugs anyway.

"I hate to say it, buddy, but nobody likes bugs! Know what I mean? What readers love is disaster stories, like why don't you write a story about this passenger airplane that catches on fire in mid-flight, and the wheels fall off so they can't land safely, and everyone on board is screaming and praying. They're gonna crash into a nearby town, a hospital or a school, something like that, and the pilot has a heart attack. You know? People love a story like that."

Pretty soon, Andy stopped coming to see Ronald. Andy kept calling him, but he no longer appeared in the yard outside Ronald's window to give him karate lessons.

Finally, Andy had a serious talk with Ronald's mom. He said he loved tutoring Ronald, the kid was a darn good kid, crazy smart, but he had just landed a new full-time job at the university advising low-achieving freshmen.

"They need my help, or they're gonna flunk out, you know? I mean, it's my dream job. Could you talk to the kid for me? Give him my best, but tell him I got more responsibilities now, right? I have to move on. Tell him to stay positive!"

Ronald's mother told Ronald that Andy had resigned as his tutor. She would place an ad for a new one.

Ronald told her not to bother.

Ronald quit wearing the school uniform.

He told Cook, "You don't have to call me Buddy anymore."

Ronald called up Ann.

"You guys are right. I hate my happy ending. Know what? I tore it into little bits. I'm gonna write a new story! You're gonna love it!"

CHAPTER 25: YABA BABBY BOOK, A NEW AND BETTER STORY BY RONALD MATTHEWS

You know that last story, the one with the happy ending? That never happened. That was just a dream the boy had. When he woke up from his stupid dream, the boy was still—almost—a house fly. He had the abdomen and thorax of a house fly, and he had a house fly's wings. But at least his head was still human—mostly. Also, because he was poisonous, the boy still smelled bad, so Melody didn't like him much. She definitely didn't want him to be her boyfriend. What did she need a boyfriend for? Her dad, Dr. Fabber, the renowned entomologist, was still wandering around in the grass forest trying to avoid being eaten by predatory insects. Melody was still looking for him and trying to figure out how to make the ring do its magic. She was not having any success. Also, it was starting to get cold at night because it was autumn. Winter was coming. Know what happens when it gets below freezing at night? Insects and tiny people DIE, that's what!

As usual, Insect Boy was buzzing around in the wizard's back yard, looking for food. He ate soft, wet, disgusting stuff that I won't even mention. Houseflies are not picky about what they eat. Take my word for it.

This is the unfortunate and rotten thing that happened to the boy. One day, the wizard left his back door open because he had to take the trash out. While the door was open, the boy flew right into the wizard's house because it was warm in there. Like all the other insects, the boy was getting weaker because of the cold. He flew into the wizard's warm house, and the next thing he knew, he was buzzing around like a little lost airplane in the wizard's kitchen, landing on walls and cupboards. Then he smelled something. Oh, my goodness! Sugar! Flies can't resist anything sweet.

The wizard loved grape soda. He was practically addicted to the stuff. Every day, the wizard drank six cans of it. Sometimes seven. Right on top of the kitchen counter, not far from the sink, was an open can of grape soda, and some of that soda was in a puddle on the counter. The wizard must have slopped a few drops and didn't clean up his mess. Oh, it smelled good! So far as the boy was concerned, it was a little purple lake of delicious, irresistible sugar! He landed on the counter beside the puddle and used his proboscis to suck up a tiny drop of the soda pop. I forgot to mention, because of the magic, because of the wizard's curse, the boy was still changing. He still had a human head, most of one, but now he had a proboscis too, where his mouth used to be.

Oh, my goodness gracious, that sugary soda pop was good! And then—disaster!

This next part of this story is pretty scary. I mean it. So, brace yourself. In fact, if you are a nervous sort of person, quit reading right now!

I think I explained a while ago that the magic ring, the one that Melody stole from the wizard, contained the spirit of an evil magician. Long ago, and I mean centuries ago, the spirit had been captured by a good wizard and trapped inside the ring. The ring wound up in a box. Try to imagine how boring it would be to be trapped inside a ring and left inside a box for centuries. When the evil wizard, the modern one, after years of searching, obtained that box and put the magic ring on his finger, the ring was happy. It was like getting out of prison when you have been stuck down in a dark dungeon for so long you can't even remember what blue sky looks like.

The spirit's name was Yaba Babby Book. Not really, but I do not dare reveal the spirit's true name because it would be dangerous. Extremely. The real name of a spirit, pronounced slowly and accurately, can cause the spirit to materialize. I cannot be held responsible for what might happen next. I just want to say, unless you know what you are doing, never ever say the real name of a spirit. Don't even whisper it. Don't even think it!

The wizard knew the spirit's real name. He put the ring on his finger and pronounced the name, slowly and carefully, and after that, he had power over the ring. The ring had to do what he said.

The ring liked the situation at first, because anything was better than being stuck in that dark box. He liked doing evil in service to the wizard. The spirit inside the ring enjoyed following orders, enchanting people, shrinking them until they were no bigger than ants. That was fun!

But at a certain point, the spirit in the ring got a little tired of being bossed around by the wizard. Also, there was the fact that the wizard had gone back on the deal. When the wizard had first put the ring on his finger and whispered the ring's true name, the wizard had made a promise. For one entire year, the ring would serve him. When that year was finished, the wizard would free the spirit.

Oh, to be free!

But what happened? The year came and went. The wizard did not free the spirit. He acted as if he couldn't even remember the deal. A second year went by, and then a third. Clearly, the wizard was NEVER going to honor his side of the bargain. He intended to keep Yaba Babby Book trapped in the ring forever!

That was why, when Melody showed up one night and stole the ring, the ring let it happen. Why not? By then, he was sick and tired of the wizard. Who did the wizard think he was, a bigshot? Without the ring and its magical power, the wizard was nothing! Maybe it would be more fun to be owned by this girl. Besides, she didn't even know his real name, so she couldn't force him to do magic.

The ring went along with Melody for a while. It helped her find the magic suit of invulnerability and then shrank her and the suit to the size of an insect so she could wander around in the wizard's back yard searching for her father. But now it had changed its mind. The girl wasn't evil. All she ever wanted to do was nice stuff. What fun was it to be a magic ring on the thumb of a kind person? Boring! Spirits trapped inside magic rings get all twisted and mean. They love being evil! The ring began to miss the wizard.

I know what you're thinking. You're wondering why the girl had power over grasshoppers. Wasn't that because of the magic ring? In fact, no. The grasshoppers just seemed to like Melody.

The ring was stuck on Melody's thumb, and winter was coming on, so it started thinking maybe it could renegotiate its deal with the wizard. The ring started sending dreams into the wizard's head when the wizard was asleep. He was sleeping a lot because he was depressed. I mean, think about it. Who was he without any powers? Just a fat bald man that nobody liked.

The ring sent lots of bad dreams into the wizard's head. Nightmares. In these dreams, which seemed very real, all the people that the wizard had turned into bugs came back, seeking revenge. They invaded the wizard's house, poured under the doors, attacked him—thousands of ants, spiders, centipedes, beetles! The wizard often woke up feeling sick, covered in sweat, trembling. He would turn on the lights and check his hands and arms and legs to be sure they were not covered in bugs. Every day, he rubbed insecticide all over his arms and legs and the back of his neck.

The good side of it was that the dreams told the wizard who the person was who had robbed him. Not another evil wizard or even an—ugh! —good wizard. He had been robbed by a little girl! The daughter of Henry Fabber, the entomologist he had trapped in a jar and kept in his basement. Oh, it was so embarrassing! To be robbed of his magic, to have his powers stolen—by a girl!

Every night, the wizard dreamed about the girl. Oh, how he hated her! If only he had his magic ring back on his finger, he would turn her into a frog! No, into a toad! No, into a worm! And then he would cut the worm into pieces!

Every day, the evil wizard crawled on his hands and knees in his back yard, looking in the grass for that girl who had stolen the ring. He had to find her!

One night, his dreams told the wizard a secret. The girl had a friend, a buddy, a Fly Boy. He vaguely remembered enchanting the boy, cursing him. At the time, he had been in love with the boy's mother. Not really in love. He had desired the woman, and the boy had been in the way, so he had cursed him, shrunk him. Then he had erased the woman's memories of the boy.

But he had wearied of that stupid woman.

The wizard was not really capable of love. He was too evil.

Besides, who cared about a stupid boy and his stupid mother? It was that girl, Melody, who stole his ring! He had to find her! Every day, the wizard crawled on his knees in his back yard, looking for her.

And then, one day, a miracle happened. The wizard took out his trash, came back inside, closed his door, entered his kitchen—and saw a fly land on his counter right beside the kitchen sink. Wait ... it was not an ordinary fly. Now the fly was slurping up spilled grape soda. He ought to get his swatter and smash it. But hold on a second, that was definitely no ordinary fly. It had a—mostly—human head! It was the boy in his dreams, the friend of the girl! The wizard trembled with excitement. Moving slowly and quietly so as not to disturb the fly, the wizard took a drinking glass out of his cupboard and placed it over the fly.

By the time the fly realized it was in danger, it was too late. It was a prisoner!

That night, his dreams told the wizard what to do next.

The next day, right after he ate his breakfast, the wizard put Fly Boy into a jar with a screw-top lid and carried it out into the back yard. In a loud voice, he announced he knew the little girl who stole his ring could hear him. "Look up here, thief! See what I got in this here jar!" He shook the jar until the boy banged into the sides. "It's your pal, Fly Boy. If you don't bring me my ring right now, I'm gonna rip off his wings! You hear? I'm gonna yank off his head! Listen good, girl! Then I'll flush the whole mess down the toilet. You listening? Return my ring! I'm gonna count to a hundred. Gimme back my ring! You have my word. Return the ring! And no harm will befall you! Put my ring right here on the toe of my shoe. I swear, Fly Boy will be released unharmed. I promise on my mama's life. No harm will befall you or this here boy! I promise I will restore you and your daddy—oh yes, I know who your daddy is! You, your daddy, and Fly Boy here! All three of you! I'll return all of you to normal size. I swear! I promise! No harm to you, never! On my mama's life! Gimme back the ring! Or else Fly Boy here dies!"

Down in the grass forest, Melody heard the wizard's voice. It sounded like thunder. It sounded like the voice of God!

"ONE HUNDRED, NINETY-NINE, NINETY-EIGHT, NINETY-SEVEN...."

When the count got down to TWENTY, the tiny magic ring appeared on the toe of the wizard's shoe. It sparkled in the sunlight. The wizard looked down, saw it, and smiled.

On the toe of the wizard's shoe, the ring began to expand. It grew larger and larger, and brighter and brighter, until it was hard to look at it because it was so bright.

The wizard reached down and picked up the magic ring. It was so hot to the touch he almost dropped it.

He spoke to the ring, "I swear to you, Yaba Babby Book, I will never remove you from my finger again! Never, never, never!"

The wizard pushed the ring back onto his finger. Immediately, he felt better, taller, stronger. He felt his magic return to him. He felt it pour into his veins and light up his brain.

And then, he stomped all over the nearby grass in hopes of smashing the girl, Melody.

The wizard felt so wild, so triumphant and evil, that he threw the glass jar containing Fly Boy as hard as he could against the wall of his house. The jar burst into a million pieces.

Only a fool makes a deal with a wizard. The wizard didn't even have a mama. Not anymore. That was a big fat lie. She had been dead for years. Besides, he never loved her in the first place. He was too evil.

That night, under a clear, dark sky filled with stars, the wizard stood in the middle of his back yard and performed a spell. He whispered to his magic ring, pronouncing the syllables of its true name, and then he spread his arms wide and threw back his head and uttered the words of a freezing spell.

The sky darkened. Heavy, dense, black clouds appeared and blocked out the light of the stars. Thunder rumbled. An icy wind began to blow from the north. Cold rain began to fall, and then hard, icy pellets of sleet. And then snow. Snow and ice fell upon the back yard until they buried every blade of grass and killed every single insect. The ants, the centipedes and spiders, the beetles and moths, the crickets and grasshoppers began to move slowly, and then more slowly. Buried beneath a foot of snow, they ceased to move at all. The snow fell and fell, icy flake after icy flake. It fell until the entire back yard was just a field of cold white death.

The End

Or is it????

CHAPTER 26: THE BOY WHO CAN'T BE TOUCHED

Andy went to a party given by his new boss, the associate director of Student Services at the university. Ten minutes after arriving, he managed to position himself next to a young woman who had all the qualities he most admired in young women: a nice figure, long blond hair, and blue eyes. Andy examined her long legs and her blue eyes and developed an instant crush. He introduced himself. The young woman looked at him without much interest, but at least she did not turn and walk away, which was all the encouragement Andy needed. He was just about to start telling her about his physical training program and his black belt in karate, when it suddenly occurred to him that she might be the type of young woman who loved kittens and little kids, so he told her about his former gig tutoring this sweet boy who was allergic to everything. The young woman perked up, and he congratulated himself for winning her attention. She loved hearing about the kid. Andy said, "And get this. The kid's mom is one of the most famous criminal defense lawyers in Chicago. She works for all the big gangsters and murderers."

When she heard about Ronald's mom, the young woman became even more interested. She started interrupting and asking Andy questions and even touched him on the wrist two times, so he was pretty sure she was falling for him.

"Wait a second," she said. "I know someone who would LOVE to meet you."

Andy wasn't thrilled by this news.

It turned out Blue Eyes knew a reporter for a big Chicago paper, and guess what, he was also at the party, right over there. Andy had no desire to share Blue Eyes with some stupid reporter, but what could he do? She yelled at the reporter and signaled him to come over.

"Billy!"

Andy hated Billy on sight. On general principles, he hated men with beards, plus this guy was wearing a turtleneck. Andy hated men who wore turtlenecks, and what was Turtleneck holding in his hand? A pipe! This guy was the kind of dork who wore a turtleneck AND had a stupid beard AND smoked a pipe.

The dork came over to them.

"What's up, babe?"

He called her "babe"! Worse, he kissed Blue Eyes, just a little peck on the lips, but still! The kiss irritated Andy so much, it was all he could do not to karate chop the guy.

Not only did the dork have a beard and wear a turtleneck, he had a paunch. Andy was sure this guy had never done a sit-up in his entire life. The whole idea a girl as pretty as Blue Eyes could be with a dork made Andy want to scream.

It turned out Blue Eyes and this jerk were ENGAGED!

Andy realized he didn't have a chance in the romance department, not with Blue Eyes. He told the dork, "Nice to meet you, buddy," and started scanning the crowd in hopes of finding another pretty woman the right age. A skinny brunette wearing bellbottoms was standing over by the door all by herself, sipping beer from a cup, looking bored as if she was already thinking about leaving. She seemed a perfect target, but before Andy could go over there and make a move, Blue Eyes trapped him. She reached out, grabbed his wrist, and held on. He couldn't escape. She was telling the dork about this kid Andy tutored, this unfortunate boy who could never leave his room because of his condition.

"And—get this, honey—the kid's mom is Margaret Matthews, the Lawyer for the Mob."

The next thing Andy knew, he was being interrogated by the dork. The reporter wanted to know all about Ronald. Andy had to stand there and answer all his stupid questions, and by the time the dork drifted away, the pretty brunette over by the door was gone.

The next morning, Mrs. Matthews got a phone call at her office from a reporter. The newspaper would like to interview her, do an entire feature article on her, because she was such a successful criminal attorney and defended murderers and gangsters. The public was very interested in gangsters and murderers and the people who defended them, and in this case their defender was a woman. Mrs. Matthews was carving out an impressive career for herself in the man's world of the legal profession. The public needed to know exciting stuff like that. Could the reporter come to see her? For a special story like this one, the reporter would like to do the interview face to face and bring a photographer. Maybe they could do the interview at her home. Would that be OK? They could interview her at her office downtown, sitting in front of a wall full of law books, but a picture of her sitting in her office would be trite, a cliché really. The story could be lots bigger and there would be more personal interest if it could be done in her home. By the way, was it true she had a disabled son she cared for? The readers would LIKE it that she was a tough, experienced, hardnose defense attorney, but they would LOVE it if they found out she also had this soft, domestic, feminine side and was a loving mother to her special needs son.

All this sounded pretty good to Mrs. Matthews.

Two days later, as agreed, the reporter and a photographer arrived at Mrs. Matthews' house. The reporter was a nice-looking young man with a well-trimmed beard. He was wearing a turtleneck and a tweed jacket with elbow patches, and he smelled of pipe tobacco. Mrs. Matthews liked him. She gave him a tour of her house. It was a pretty cool house, even if she did say so herself. She introduced the reporter to her housekeeper, Cook. The photographer trailed behind them and took pictures of everything, including a photo of Cook. He took pictures of Mrs. Matthews in her kitchen pretending to cook something on the stove, even though in real life that would never happen because the housekeeper did all the cooking, and pictures of Mrs. Matthews in the living room, posed attractively on a sofa. Oh, by the way, asked the reporter, could they also meet the kid, the special needs boy? "Would that be OK?"

Mrs. Matthews took them to Ronald's wing of the house. They couldn't enter Ronald's room of course. It was a hermetically sealed room because of the boy's condition, but the photographer could take photos of the kid through the window in Ronald's door. Mrs. Matthews posed with the telephone and pretended to tell Ronald what was going on even though Ronald already knew.

Ronald was looking spiffy. He was wearing his school uniform, at least the jacket and shirt and trousers. Unfortunately, he had refused to wear the tie. He was barefoot, but not to worry. The photographer would make sure not to photograph his feet.

Mrs. Matthews said to the phone which was connected to Ronald, "Honey, these men are from the newspaper. They're doing a story on me. You don't mind if they take your picture, do you?" Ronald posed while the photographer took several photos. When the photographer finished, the reporter got on the phone and asked Ronald, "Where do you go to school? Public or private? Can I call you Ronald? Oh wow, you don't go out, never? Homeschooled, huh? I hear you're allergic to everything, man oh man. That must be tough. So, like what would happen if you stepped outside? Amazing. Is it getting worse, you think, your condition? What do the doctors say? Wow. How many times you been in the hospital, that many? Wow, to the ICU and everything, wow. How you feeling today, like what is a normal day for you? Can you eat regular food or ...? You've been living here in this room your whole entire life? Amazing. You've never seen a mall? A mall is like this huge building with a bunch of stores in it. What about going for a drive in a car? Wow. You've never gone to the circus, the movies, nothing like that? Can't even watch TV. It makes you nauseous, wow. But you like to read." The reporter was using his shoulder to hold the phone to his ear because he needed both hands to write Ronald's answers in his notebook. "No one can go in there with you, not since your last trip to the ICU, not even your mom? Nobody can touch you or anything? Protective clothing. Wow. You are one super brave kid. How do you keep your spirits up?"

While the interview with Ronald continued, the photographer snapped pictures and talked to Mrs. Matthews. She said talking to Ronald on the phone through a window was exactly like talking to one of her clients in jail. In the county jail, they had that same set up, the accused criminals on one side of a window, and the attorneys on the other side. Because of her job, she visited the jail so often that she was on a first name basis with all the cops.

After the reporter thanked Ronald for being so cooperative and the photographer took one more picture of Ronald, they went back to the living room. Cook served them coffee cake. The reporter asked Mrs. Matthews questions about the famous criminals she had defended. She reminded him about attorney-client privilege. He said probably the story would run next weekend.

"Thank you so much, Mrs. Matthews. We really appreciate it. This is gonna be awesome."

In due course, the story ran in the features section of the paper, except it turned out Mrs. Matthews was not the focus. Ronald was. The feature article included a big picture of Ronald inside his hermetically sealed room sitting cross-legged and barefoot on his bed, a picture of him looking out his window at the outdoors where he was never allowed to go, and a smaller picture of his mom, the attorney who defended criminals, talking to him using the phone that was exactly like the one in the jail.

At the top of the page, a huge headline said:

THE BOY WHO CAN'T BE TOUCHED.

CHAPTER 27: DR. FABBER AND THE ANTS, A STORY BY RONALD MATTHEWS

After escaping from the wizard's basement, Dr. Fabber explored the back yard. In one way, it was the most awe-inspiring experience of his life because he got to observe his beloved insects up close and personal, but in another way, it was terrifying. If he was not extremely careful, one of the predatory insects might eat him. Dr. Fabber was afraid to go to sleep. He was OK for the first day, and not too bad for the second, but by the third he was stumbling around the grass forest, barely able to keep his eyes open.

He had another big problem. What was he going to eat?

For three long hungry days, Dr. Fabber starved, but then he got a lucky break. It will not seem a lucky break to most people, but that is because most people aren't starving. Dr. Fabber came upon the corpse of a dead ant. Its abdomen had burst open revealing the soup inside.

I know. Yuck! But wait.

This is something about ants that a lot of people don't know. They have a communal stomach. Let's say an ant is wandering around the grass forest doing his job, foraging for something edible it can drag back to the nest to feed the ant babies, and it gets hungry. At that point, the foraging ant is like a car running out of gas. It needs more fuel! When it sees another ant, it runs up to it and pounds on its head with its antennae. This is a signal that means: feed me! The ant getting pounded will vomit up a cup of delicious soup from out of its stomach and the hungry ant will slurp it up. Then it will run back to work, not even bothering to say thank you. Ants share food with one another in this way all the time. For them, it isn't the least bit disgusting.

Dr. Fabber was one of the greatest entomologists in the world so, of course, he knew all about the communal stomach of ants. He devoured the contents of the dead ant's stomach. Yummy! You are probably feeling sick just reading about this, but so far as Dr. Fabber was concerned, it was the most delicious stew he had ever eaten. He hadn't eaten a thing in days!

Then—don't forget how long he had been awake—with his stomach full, he couldn't help it. He yawned and stretched. His eyes grew heavy. He lay down and fell asleep right there at the foot of a blade of grass.

One minute, Dr. Fabber was having a nice dream. He was tall, normal-sized, back home with his beloved daughter Melody. The next thing he knew, he was jerked awake, caught in the mandibles of a patrol ant who took him for a nest inhabitant, because he had the nest smell now.

I had better explain about nest smell. Patrol ants do not have great vision. They depend on their sense of smell. If they come across something that smells edible, they grab it, drag it back to the nest, and feed it to the ant babies. If the discovery is too big and heavy for one ant to handle, the ant runs back to the nest to get help. A whole team of ants drag the discovery back to the nest. Sometimes, though, one of the foraging ants encounters another insect (not an ant) that has the nest smell. This may surprise you, but ant nests contain non-ants. They live down there in the nest with the ants and are never bothered by the guards because they have the nest smell. But there is a downside. They can't escape. Let's say one of these lazy good-for-nothings escapes the nest. The moment a patrol ant comes across them, it will seize them and drag them right back to the nest. So far as the patrol ant is concerned, if you smell like the nest, it's their job to drag you back where you belong. Basically, once you smell like you belong in the nest, you're never going to get out.

That is what happened to Dr. Fabber. Because he had eaten all the contents of the dead ant's stomach, and even spilled some on his shirt, he had the nest smell. A foraging ant discovered him, concluded he was one of the non-ant inhabitants of the nest, grabbed him, dragged him all the way back to the nest, and turned him over to a guard ant, who carried him down into the darkness of the nest and left him down there.

Dr. Fabber found out he could explore the tunnels without interference, but if he got anywhere near the entrance, a guard would seize him and carry him deep into the nest and leave him down there. Escape was impossible. There were too many guards.

Dr. Fabber had plenty to eat, but there wasn't much variety. Ant babies, also called larvae, look like barrels—barrels with teeth.

They are fed by the patrol ants. This is an interesting fact about ants. Adult ants can't chew their food because they don't have any teeth. To turn their captures into food, they cut them up and feed them to the ant babies. The ant babies do have teeth, but they lack legs and can't go hunting for themselves. The ant babies chew up the food and turn it into soup. Remember what I said about the communal stomach? When an ant gets hungry, it pounds on an ant baby until the baby disgorges soup. That is what Dr. Fabber did, too. He pounded on an ant baby until it spewed up soup and then he ate it, using his hands as a cup.

A guy can get tired of eating soup day after day, but what are you going to do? Dr. Fabber did not like to get too far from the nursery where the ant babies were because he was afraid he might get lost in the maze of tunnels and never find the nursery again. Then he would probably starve to death.

It was boring down there in the dark. There isn't any light in an ant nest. The ants don't care because they have an excellent sense of smell. Dr. Fabber had a sense of smell, but it was nothing compared to the ants' sense of smell. He had to feel his way along the tunnels of the nest and try not to bump into anyone.

He soon lost all sense of time. Was it day? Was it night? He had no way of knowing. How long had he been in the nest? A week? A month? The only way he had of estimating time was to count his sleeps. When he got tired, he found a quiet nook and fell asleep.

Probably the space between his sleeps was a day long. Probably.

After a while, it was hard for Dr. Fabber to know when he was awake and when he was asleep. Was he awake? Or was he dreaming? One thing he discovered, if he could see, then he was dreaming. But then a scary thing began to happen. Even Dr. Fabber's dreams began to take place in the dark.

Did his eyes even work anymore?

Dr. Fabber began to feel sorry for himself. How was he ever going to escape? Was he going to have to live in the dark with nothing to eat but ant soup for the rest of his life? Was he going to die down here?

Probably that would have been his fate, except for an amazing event that changed everything.

An enemy queen arrived at the nest entrance and fought her way into the nest. These enemy queens are lazy, but they possess fighting spirit. They have no interest in digging a nest of their own. Instead, they invade another queen's nest and take it over. Invader queens are bigger than normal ants. They are ferocious fighters, and the guards cannot stop them. If a guard attempts to block the path of the invading queen, she snips its head off with her jaws. She keeps it up, murdering guard after guard, getting deeper and deeper into the nest until she finds the resident queen. Then she hops on top of her and saws off her head!

The invader becomes the new queen. People who don't know much about insects probably imagine ant queens have to run everything, order the other ants to do this and that, but in fact a queen is just an egg layer. Once she is installed in the throne room, she starts pumping out eggs and cares for them until they hatch and turn into larvae. The invader queen feeds her first batch of larvae with pieces of her dead rival until the larvae turn into adult ants. After that, she does not have to do a darn thing except produce more eggs. Her new ants take care of her. Some of them take care of the eggs. Some feed the larvae. Some guard the nest. Some run outside and forage for food. Adult ants just know what to do because they have instincts. No one has to order them to do it.

At this point, you may be wondering what happened to all the old ants. Well, I will tell you. After their queen was dead, they lost all sense of purpose. They wandered around bumping into one another like zombies. They deserted their own nest.

Pretty soon, except for the invader queen and her eggs, the entire nest was empty. Dr. Fabber groped his way higher and higher, wondering what happened.

"Where are all the guards?"

As he climbed, he heard what sounded like thunder. Someone outside was counting backward. It was the voice of the wizard!

"ONE HUNDRED, NINETY-NINE, NINETY-EIGHT, NINETY-SEVEN …."

By the time Dr Fabber got to the entrance of the nest and could see daylight, the count was down to TWENTY-THREE, TWENTY-TWO, TWENTY-ONE, TWENTY!

Dr. Fabber stood in the entrance of the nest. He could see him now, the wizard, a giant so big he practically blocked out the sky.

"I SWEAR, YABA BABBY BOOK, I WILL NEVER REMOVE YOU FROM MY FINGER AGAIN! NEVER, NEVER, NEVER!"

Hours later, it was nighttime, and Dr. Fabber heard it again, the thunderous voice of the wizard, casting a spell. Clouds moved in overhead, hiding the stars. A cold wind began to blow. Snowflakes as big as dinner plates began to spin down out of the darkness.

CHAPTER 28: THE SPACE PROGRAM HAS A PROBLEM

Betsey Bottom was a low-level employee in the glamorous space program. Unfortunately, her job was not glamorous. Every day from nine to five, she sat at a desk in the press office armed with a pair of scissors and paged through newspapers and magazines looking for stories about the space program. When Betsey found a story of this type, she carefully cut it from the newspaper or magazine, labelled it and put it into one of two piles, positive or critical. For example, if Betsey found an editorial that claimed the astronauts were the handsomest and brightest and most patriotic of all Americans, she put it into the positive file. On the other hand, if she found an article about how an astronaut got arrested for drunken driving, it went straight into the critical pile. But there never would be an article like that because, if any astronaut did get arrested, officers of the government would soon arrive at the offending police station and see that those charges were dropped.

When Betsey got hired for her job, the positive pile was always much taller than the negative pile. Some days, every single article that Betsey clipped landed on the positive file. Every single one! But lately, the negative pile was growing. The positive pile was still much taller, but the growth of the negative pile was worrisome, and not just to Betsey.

On this particular day, the first thing that Betsey had to do was attend a meeting of everyone in the press office. Betsey's boss paced back and forth in front of his staff and declared, "We have a problem."

The problem was that negative pile! It was growing! They had to do something about it!

At one point, the boss actually glared at Betsey, as if the growth of the negative pile was her fault.

In Betsey's opinion, the problem was not the space program, which was efficient and heroic and glamorous and scientific and important. The problem was certainly not her fault either. The problem was the public.

When the astronaut, Neil Armstrong, set foot on the moon, the public went wild. The entire world went insane with happiness and excitement.

"America has put a man on the MOON!"

People were dancing in front of their TVs. People were weeping and praising science. Politicians were not only toasting the space program with champagne; they were throwing money at it. The boss said the only thing that could possibly happen that would get more positive PR than Neil Armstrong setting foot on the moon would be the return of Jesus Christ.

The second trip to the moon was not quite so popular. It was popular, but there were a few small but possibly alarming trends. Although the space program continued to have very high approval ratings, very high indeed, there were ... concerns. For one thing, while everyone polled knew who Neil Armstrong was, the two astronauts who went with him never became especially famous. You could ask the man on the street to name them, and nine out of ten people would scratch their heads.

Although the second mission to the moon could not possibly have gone any better, excitement about the space program dropped slightly. Worse, when polled, nine out of ten people could not name even ONE of the astronauts in the second mission.

Also, the poll revealed American teenagers (an important demographic) were beginning to lose interest in the program. They were not downright hostile, but they showed a marked preference for rock stars like the Beatles. The Beatles were scruffy, badly dressed, long-haired hippies, and yet they were preferred by young people to astronauts. Preferred by a significant margin. This seemed contrary to reason because the astronauts were clean-cut, healthy, well educated, brave, and patriotic. Every one of them was a married man with children. They were college graduates. They had crew cuts for heaven's sake. The poll asked, "Which would you rather be, an astronaut or a rock star?" Seven out of ten teenagers replied, "Rock Star."

Betsey's boss said this was unacceptable.

Then, something unfortunate and very unexpected happened.

The third mission to the moon failed spectacularly. The failure was certainly not the fault of anyone in the press office. The spaceship had gotten half-way to the moon when something went wrong with it. The whole world watched on TV. People love to watch a disaster as it unfolds. It was a close thing, very close, but fortunately the astronauts inside the capsule did not die.

The ship had to abandon its mission. It had to make a U-turn and return to Earth, mission not accomplished. The press office had done everything possible to emphasize the heroism of the astronauts and the brilliance of the scientists and engineers who had figured out how to keep the astronauts alive despite the accident and get them back home safe and sound, but the public learned the wrong lesson. The space program did not always succeed. And really, when you thought about it, what was the point of sending more and more astronauts to the moon at incredible expense on dangerous missions?

Already, certain rabblerousers were travelling the country declaring we were wasting too much money on the space program when we should be taking care of our problems down here on Earth— poverty and racism for example.

The trend-line was clear as day. The space program was in trouble.

Betsey's boss got red in the face and waved his arms. He said they needed to do a better job. That negative trend line had to be reversed! Or every blessed one of them could start looking for another job!

Back in her cubicle, paging through the latest newspapers, Betsey came across the big feature story about Ronald, The Boy Who Can't Be Touched.

Betsey got an idea.

A week later, three representatives of the space program came to visit Mrs. Matthews and Ronald.

CHAPTER 29: THE SUIT

It was springtime, and Max was on the phone. Ronald had a new phone number, an unlisted one, because otherwise complete strangers would be calling him every ten minutes.

Max loved this whole thing. Ronald did not love this whole thing. He wished he could go back to his peaceful, normal, quiet life. Max was saying that a custom-made space suit is practically as good as an exoskeleton.

"But it needs to look cool. Know what I mean? When it arrives, you gotta paint flames on it, know what I mean? Equip it with a stinger or sharp claws or something. And compound eyes! Make it look badass. Like a praying mantis! Or OK, you probably want to look like a superhero, am I right? No problem. It could be painted blue and red like Superman. And definitely wear a cape! Or bumblebee-stripe it. No, wait! Black, like Batman. Black would be the coolest. I recommend black. And what about a pair of antennae bobbing from the helmet? And carry a sword! Oh, my god! It would be *insanely* cool if you make a big entrance in your suit, and everyone sees you for the first time, and they, like, GASP and jump back, terrified. Peeing their pants! Because you are a total super villain! That would be WICKED cool. Know what I mean?"

Max yelped because Ann was right beside him, pinching him because she wanted to talk to Ronald. She said, "Quit hogging the phone!"

Ann got on the phone.

"Don't listen to my stupid brother. Are you OK?"

Ronald told her he was nervous about taking a walk in a park with a whole bunch of cameras watching.

"What if I fall over or ...?"

"Don't be silly. You aren't gonna fall over. Quit worrying. Worrying never gets anyone anywhere."

Ann was rather pleased about this whole thing because, at school, she was much more popular than usual, all because of the fact she was considered to be Ronald's girlfriend. She was not really Ronald's girlfriend. They were just good friends. Ronald would probably get mad if he heard anyone thought she was his girlfriend, but he did not know. Ann felt she was not doing anything wrong because she did not actually claim to be Ronald's girlfriend. That was just a rumor that got started and kept going. She never bothered to put an end to it, because why should she? Other girls, including popular girls who never normally talked to her, told her it must be really sad when you can't even touch your boyfriend, can't kiss him or anything like that, can't even hold his hand, but it was obvious to Ann that the other girls thought her romance with The Boy Who Can't Be Touched was super exciting. Those girls were popular, but they didn't have famous boyfriends, did they?

Ronald said he was thinking about calling the whole thing off.

"Maybe I'll just refuse to even wear the darn suit. Refuse any more stupid interviews, until finally they quit bothering me. They can find someone else to pester."

Ann said, "Ronald, you need to relax. I've been thinking about stuff you can do in the park, like go on the swings. Me and Max can push you."

Ann loved the idea of appearing on TV with millions of people watching. She had already selected the outfit she would wear. She would accessorize it with sunglasses, even if it was a cloudy day, so she would look like a movie star.

"You could look at flowers and stuff, pose for photos beside a big tree. How easy is that?" Ann confided that she was just a little worried about being photographed with Ronald, standing beside him when he was wearing his space suit. "I heard the TV cameras make you look heavier. Did you ever hear that? Like they add ten pounds, no one knows why. You don't think I'm too plump, do you?"

She waited for Ronald to tell her she looked fine, but he didn't say anything.

Ann said, "Maybe they should rethink the whole park idea. If you ask me, it would be way better if we go to the mall. We can buy clothes and records and stuff, especially if the space program pays for everything. I mean, think about it. I bet you anything the stores will *give us stuff* just for the free publicity!"

Ronald said he was nervous about being stared at by lots of people.

"In that suit, you will be almost invisible. It will be like you aren't even there because all anyone will be able to see is the space suit." Suddenly she laughed.

"What's so funny?"

"Wouldn't it be hilarious if I wore the suit? I could wear the suit and pretend I'm you. Who would know? That would be so hilarious!"

Ronald said they would just get caught.

"I'll probably need help even getting into the suit, technicians from the space program will have to help me zip it up or whatever, put the helmet on. No way could someone besides me be inside the suit."

Ann squealed.

"For Pete's sake, quit pushing! Max wants to talk to you."

Max got on the phone. He suggested when Ronald was at the park, he should do something sports related.

"Obviously, you can't play baseball wearing the suit, but maybe we could shoot baskets, you and me. We could play Horse or something." Max tried to explain the rules of Horse, but Ronald was not listening. He said he didn't want to try to shoot baskets while wearing the suit with TV cameras pointing at him.

When Ronald got done talking to his friends, he sat on his bed and felt nervous. His stomach hurt. He called up his mother, who was in her law office. He told her he was worried about the upcoming TV show.

"Why do cameras have to be there at all? Why can't I just do it with nobody watching? Like at night in the dark somewhere? They could let me test it, like, in privacy. No cameras."

Mrs. Matthews told him not to be a prima donna. She said it was too late now because they had signed the contract which stipulated Ronald would wear the suit in public in a location chosen by the space program and allow the news media approved by the space program to record the event.

"You need to relax, honey. Everything will be fine."

Ronald sighed and hung up the phone.

On the special day, four black vans pulled up to the park. The first two vans and the last one opened their doors and disgorged men in suits, three men from each van. The men were equipped with walkie talkies. Cops lined the edges of the park. It was their job to ensure that no one without an invitation could enter the park and cause a disruption of the scheduled events. A cluster of approved people, including the mayor of Chicago and his wife, were waiting to meet the boy. When everyone was where he or she was supposed to be and the police officers on the perimeter signaled the park was secure, the side door of the third van slid open and two men in suits helped the boy get out.

Ronald looked like a space man. A short one.

Six cheerleaders from a nearby school led a cheer for the Space Boy. He waved a gloved hand at the cheerleaders. He also waved at the mayor and his companions. The sun reflected off his helmet.

The mayor made a speech and presented Ronald a key to the city of Chicago. He said the boy must be the happiest boy in the world because, now he had his protective space suit, Ronald could go anywhere he wanted and be welcomed. The mayor said he and his wife were hoping to take the boy and his mother to a baseball game, the Sox or the Cubs, whichever team the boy preferred.

The key to the city proved cumbersome because it was so large. Ronald handed it to his mother, who handed it to a man in a suit, who handed it to a woman in a dress.

A famous TV reporter who worked for a national network reported that the suit was a specially modified version of the larger suits worn by the astronauts who went to the moon. Mrs. Matthews, the boy's mother, pushed him on the merry-go-round. The Boy in the Spacesuit spun in circles while the cameras whirred.

Unfortunately, the boy's friends, Max and Ann, were nowhere to be seen because the space program publicity department had decided they were insufficiently photogenic. Ann was deemed "too heavy," and Max had large visible pimples on his chin.

The famous TV reporter explained that the suit had specially made boots that allowed Ronald to walk on the grass in the park without falling over. The suit included a self-contained life support system, so he did not have to be connected to anything by a hose. Breathing purified air, he could walk around freely, almost like a normal kid. The TV reporter said this was the first time in the boy's life that he had ever experienced flowers, bushes, trees, songbirds, squirrels, and playground equipment. He said this experience must be overwhelming to him, a dream come true, and this miracle was possible only because of the generosity of the space program and the American taxpayers.

The mayor said he couldn't agree more. He and his lovely wife were just happy to be here, delighted to represent the voters of Chicago, thrilled to be included in something historical and important like this, something that made everybody watching feel good about America.

While the boy's mother pushed him on the swings, the reporter said his live on-air exclusive interview with the boy would have to be rescheduled because Ronald had signaled that something had gone wrong with the speaker inside his helmet. This was the first time the suit had been used in a public venue, so you had to expect there might be a few glitches.

The mayor said it was a great day for Chicago, a great day for America, a great day for the entire world. He said the boy was an inspiration to everyone.

The boy tottered around the park for fifteen more minutes, and then signaled he wanted to return to the van.

The TV reporter said you couldn't blame the boy. It was as if he had been living in a cave his entire life, and now he was outdoors in the sunshine. No wonder he was overwhelmed.

Two of the men in suits helped the little spaceman climb back into his van. The other men climbed into the other vans, and then all the vans drove away, while everyone, even the cops, clapped and cheered.

CHAPTER 30: THE LITTLE FLY, A STORY BY RONALD MATTHEWS

"Where'd it go?" The wizard was standing beside the bed with his fly swatter, scanning the room. He was going to kill that darn fly if it would just hold still long enough! The fly buzzed past the wizard's ear. It had that magical ability that flies have to appear— there it is! on the bedspread!—and then disappear.

The wizard's cat had followed him upstairs and was watching, hoping to eat the fly once it was dead.

The wizard thought about casting a spell to kill the fly.

He had been much too strict with himself in terms of using magic, but all that was going to change. He had feared the world and hidden himself away, but no more! He had his magic ring back, and he was going to use it! The world would soon learn to fear him!

The fly zoomed past his head, out of the bedroom, and vanished.

The cat meowed and looked at the open door of the bathroom.

The wizard entered the bathroom and closed the door. He had the fly trapped! But where was it?

For a moment, the wizard inspected himself in the mirror over the sink. He wished he had more hair. When he was a young man, he had had a lot of hair, but what had happened to it? He tilted back his head and noticed he needed to trim the hairs inside his nostrils. How stupid it was to have hair where you didn't want it, and no hair where you did want it. And he was getting fat. His belly spilled over his belt.

That was going to change!

Where was that darn fly? He pulled back the shower curtain.

The wizard could use magic to murder the fly, but to cast a proper spell that would poison the fly or at least make its wings fall off, he needed to see the fly for the entire time he chanted the words of the spell. The darn thing moved too fast. He never could see it except for a moment, and then it disappeared.

When the fly first appeared, the wizard had been doing housework. It was Saturday morning, and that was the day he did his chores. He had put a load of clothes in the washing machine in the basement and vacuumed the living room. He had washed his breakfast dishes and put them on the rack to dry. He had gone downstairs into the basement again and taken the load of wet clothes out of the washing machine and put them into the dryer. He had set the timer on the dryer and turned it on. He had come upstairs and made his bed. He had thought about lying down on the bed for a little nap while he was waiting for the bell on the dryer to start dinging. And that was when he had noticed the darn fly.

That fly deserved to die!

Soon, the wizard told himself, he would use his magic big-time, pull out all the stops, conjure up a huge palace that would be protected from flies and all other insects by magic force fields. Why was he doing housework and waiting for the dryer in the basement to ping and announce it was done drying his socks when he was the most powerful wizard in the world? It was stupid that a great man like him had to do his own laundry. He would use the ring to enslave someone and make that person do his laundry. He tried to think of someone to enslave, that pretty girl at the convenience store maybe.

He decided the fly was not even in there and opened the bathroom door. The fly zoomed past his head and vanished. The cat meowed and looked toward the stairs. Did the stupid fly go downstairs?

Did the dryer ping?

Once he'd conjured up a palace and made it insect-proof, he would enslave twenty people and they would have to do all his housework, cook his food, clean his house, everything. He would live like a king!

He descended to the first floor holding the swatter in one hand and gripping the railing with the other hand so as not to fall. The cat followed him, meowing. It wanted to be fed.

He needed to plan out his transformation. He would make himself famous and rich and powerful, the ruler of the entire world. Why not? He would rule the Northern Hemisphere AND the Southern Hemisphere!

The fly pestered him. Where did it go?

Why not a complete and total magical makeover? He would make himself handsome, tall, athletic, young. Why not? He would have the body of a great athlete and the face of a movie star. There was a mirror on the wall beside the front door. He stood in front of it and inspected himself. He had never liked his jaw; it was too weak. And his nose, it was too big. His nose was too big and his chin too little. Magic would fix all that.

The cat was in the kitchen, meowing, staring up at the cupboard where the cans of cat food were stored. Carrying the fly swatter, the wizard walked into the kitchen. Where was that darn fly?

Once he was irresistibly handsome, everyone would want to know him. Beautiful women would fall at his feet, and powerful men would want to be his friend.

He set the fly swatter down on the counter, opened a can of tuna fish, and dumped it into the cat's bowl.

The fly landed on the back of his hand. The nerve! He slapped his own hand with his free hand, but the darn fly vanished again.

He would magic himself a lot of money. He'd fill the entire basement with cash. Why not? Millions! No, billions! He'd become the richest man in Chicago, no, in the entire country! No, the whole world!

He picked up the fly swatter and looked around the kitchen for the fly. Where was it?

The fly landed on the fly swatter and then disappeared again. The wizard spun in a circle flailing at the air with the swatter.

Once he was rich and famous, he would become the Emperor of Earth. He tried to think of some amazing miracles he could perform once he was emperor. Maybe he could cause all the people in North and South Dakota to turn into ants and give the entire region back to the buffalo. He had always liked buffalos.

Mt. Rushmore! Why should it be disfigured with the heads of dead presidents? Who cared about dead presidents? He would replace all those heads with a giant statue of himself. And what about the Eiffel Tower in Paris? He had always hated that ugly thing. He would replace it with another giant statue of himself.

No, think bigger! He would make HIMSELF enormous! A giant as tall as the Statue of Liberty! Then he would make all the little people, the world's kings and presidents and dictators come and kiss the toes of his shoes. If any of them dared to refuse, he would step on them! Squish them like ants! The shoe-kissing ceremony would be shown on TV, so everyone in the entire world could watch and learn what true magnificence looks like.

The fly zoomed past him and flew into the open door of the basement.

The dryer pinged. The cat ran to the door of the basement and looked down the flight of steps.

That fly was going to die!

All the countries would have to select their most beautiful girls and send them to him to be turned into slaves. He would cast a spell on all the women in the world to make them love him. All the men would be sick with envy! The women would love him, and the men would fear him.

He would have statues of himself erected on every street corner. Each of these statues would be twenty feet tall. No, thirty! Taller than three-story buildings!

The cat meowed and started down the steps. He followed the cat. There it was, the nasty fly! Every homeowner would be required by law to hang a photo of the emperor on the wall of their living room. A large photo!

The fly zoomed past his nose. The wizard flailed at it with the swatter, missed. The cat was in front of him, on a lower step, meowing. All the celebrities would beg to be his friends. He would star in movies. He would be the hero in ALL the movies!

The fly landed on the cat. The wizard bent down to swat the fly. He missed the fly and swatted the hind end of the cat. The cat screamed, leapt straight up into the air, and attached itself to the wizard's leg.

And suddenly, just like that, the wizard lost his balance. For a moment, he was as weightless as an astronaut floating in space.

Three days later, a neighbor complained about a horrible smell coming from the wizard's house.

CHAPTER 31: MORE PIZZAZZ

Max said, "I like your ending, but I think you need to add a little more pizzazz. Like you said, the next-door neighbor notices a really bad stink. Cool. But don't stop there! After a day of smelling the stink, the neighbor can't stand it anymore. He calls the cops, tells them about the smell. Pretty soon, a patrol car parks in the wizard's driveway. The cop gets out, rings the doorbell, right?

'Open up! It's the police!' Pounds on the door!

Nobody answers, but the cop turns the knob and finds out the door isn't even locked. The smell is so horrible, it practically makes the cop toss his cookies. He goes in. Now, get this! When the cop opens the door, the cat streaks past him, runs right out of the house. Never is seen again. That's an important detail, so don't forget it. The cop comes into the house. He's got his hands over his mouth because the stink is so bad. It's making his eyes water it's so awful. The door to the basement is open. That's where the smell is coming from. This horrible stink, gushing up from the basement. The cop stands there at the top of the stairs with his hands over his mouth, and he looks down. There it is! The source of the stink. The wizard's lying there dead, with a broken neck. He's all swollen up and rotten at the foot of the stairs. Is that so cool it's sickening, or what? I mean, it would be better if he was eaten by an army of grasshoppers, but this ending is cool in a different way. And get this, are you listening? My next idea is so good, you're not gonna believe it. Are you ready?"

Ronald made a noise to indicate he was ready.

"The cat ate him! Not all of him of course, but parts. Like his big fat nose! What do you think? Is that a fantastic ending or what?"

Ronald made the noise again.

"Or it could be his eyes are missing. The cat ate his eyes!"

Ronald said he didn't want to work on the story about the pesky fly and the wizard anymore. He didn't feel that well.

"Probably when the wizard died, all his spells lost their power. That's just common sense. Those people he put under a spell and turned into insects, they go back to being normal humans again. You have to ask yourself; do they even remember what happened to them? And what about the ring? Like, does it end up in the morgue with the dead body of the wizard? This is my idea, buddy. This is my brand-new thought. Some creepy guy who works in the funeral home gets it. He's like the guy who puts makeup on the corpses or something. He steals the ring, pulls it off the finger of the dead wizard, and puts it on his own finger! Pretty soon, he feels this feeling. It's like a billion volts of electricity shooting through him, and... don't you get it? Because the ring is turning him evil!"

Ronald made the noise again.

CHAPTER 32: THE BIRD THAT FLIES THE FARTHEST

Ronald was in bed. He wasn't sure what time it was. Late probably. He opened his eyes and wondered if it had happened yet. No, probably not. He was in his room. His mouth was dry, and he needed to pee, but he didn't feel like getting out of bed. Sometimes when he woke up in the middle of the night like this it was hard to know for a while if he was still dreaming or if he was awake. The line between dreams and normal life was harder to make out in the middle of the night.

He didn't want to alarm Cook and Mom again.

Ronald was pretty sure it was happening again because he had that weird feeling. In his opinion it had already happened at least three times, so in a way he was an expert.

Obviously, he wasn't doing it right. When you sort of do it, but not really, it's kind of rude, because you make everyone around you crazy. You're supposed to do it, done, over. You're finished, and everyone else has to go on without you. In his case, he was just a kid stuck in a room so probably the world would have zero problem going about its business without him.

There were other intriguing possibilities. For example, you could do it and start your afterlife, in heaven. Or it could be purgatory. Probably it would be purgatory because he wasn't that good or that bad, just sort of in the middle. Or—and this was his favorite notion—you might wake up and discover you were at the start of a new life. You were a brand-new baby opening its eyes for the first time—

in India or China or Indonesia or somewhere. Apparently, you forgot your previous life, except once in a while you sort of remembered it or had a dream about it.

Ronald's face was hot. Not a good sign. And his nose was plugged up, so he had to breathe through his mouth. His room was dark but not completely dark. The plastic stars on the ceiling glowed, and the nightlight made everything seem dim and strange—as if the furniture was made out of ghosts.

On the previous occasions when he did it, it was like fainting. He would feel weird and then the edges of his vision turned black. The blackness irised in until all he could see was a little hole containing some of the stars on the ceiling. The hole got smaller and smaller until he couldn't see anything, just black.

Then, hours, or even days later, he would hear beeping, the monitors, and other people would be in his room, a nurse and a doctor or even two doctors. He would hear them talking—about him— and then—hours later—he would wake up again and it would be daylight and his mom would be telling him how lucky he was.

The last time it happened, Cook told him he had been officially dead for five minutes. His heart not even beating. She thought that was pretty cool. She said it was a miracle.

In Ronald's opinion, it was not as big a deal as people thought. You have to try to imagine the world without you in the middle of it. It's not that hard. His mom would probably go on with her job helping the accused criminals. And Cook—he wasn't sure what Cook would do when she didn't have to take care of him anymore. She had a son somewhere in Florida. Maybe she would go down there and live with him. The son wasn't married, but he had a dog named Rex. Ronald couldn't remember what kind of dog it was, one of those little ones that yap. That's what Cook said anyway.

It was a lot like fainting when you thought about it.

It sort of seemed as if you ought to get lessons because otherwise how can you be sure you're doing it right? For example, when you're getting pretty close to it, other people think that's when you should be wise and say profound things, the meaning of life, that sort of thing. But in fact, your head is just full of the usual weird stuff, and you don't feel like talking.

Another idea—you do it, done, but now you are a ghost. Ronald liked that idea. Probably when you are a ghost, you are invisible. It sounds a little boring though. You just drift around invisible, spying on people? And they don't even know you are there. If he was a ghost, he would like to be noticed, he would like to be scary. You know, *Boo!*

Probably he should be thinking about Max and Ann and Mary Margaret. And about his mom— his mom especially—and his dad. His dad had sent him another book, a big fat book called *Birds of the World* with lots of pictures. It was a pretty cool book.

Another book he got from his dad was *The Adventures of Tom Sawyer*. There was this cool scene when Huck and Tom take off, run away, but then they come back and everyone in town is at the church, and everyone is bawling. The preacher is up there behind the pulpit talking and waving his arms. What's going on? Finally, the boys realize it is their own funeral! The whole town thinks they must have drowned!

It would be pretty cool to watch your own funeral. Ronald wondered, if the ghost thing was true, maybe everyone got to see that. You just float around at your own funeral and look down at all the mourners, your friends and relatives and everyone. You get to see if anyone is crying. That would be cool, but also sad, especially if you couldn't say goodbye, take it easy, it's OK.

The bird book was full of cool information. For example, you would think nobody would want to mess with an eagle, but according to the book, crows will gang up on them—it's called a murder of crows. They hate eagles. But the eagles can escape. They just fly higher and higher until the crows have to give up. Eagles can fly really high, but they don't hold the world record for altitude. The bird that does have the record is Ruppell's Griffon Vulture, which has been observed flying at an altitude of 37,OOO feet, more than seven miles up. At best, an eagle can only get up to 20,000 feet.

Of all the birds in the world, the bird that flies the farthest is the Bar-Tailed Godwit. It flies all the way from Alaska to New Zealand, almost 7000 miles without a single rest. What does a bird like that think about as it flies all by itself across so much sky? Does it feel like a ghost? Ronald thought he would like to be a cool bird like that, a high-flying, long-traveling bird that can fly forever.

That night at 2 AM, Cook said, "I'm a little worried about your temperature. I better take your blood pressure again."

"I don't feel real anymore. I think I'm turning into an insect. Or a bird."

"Don't talk like that!"

That was the last thing Ronald said to anyone.

An hour later, at 3 AM, Cook woke up Mrs. Matthews.

"He's having another bad one. You better get up. I just called for the ambulance."

While Mrs. Matthews was getting dressed, Cook said, "We knew this might happen."

At the hospital, Ronald disappeared into a special operating room.

At dawn, the sun came up, and the two women were exhausted.

"What is it again?" Mrs. Matthews asked. "What do they call it, an experimental what?"

"Bone marrow transplant." Cook tried to explain the procedure to Mrs. Matthews.

"They have to destroy his bad cells first and … and then they'll put in good ones. Oh, I don't know. We knew this might happen. All we can do is wait."

Mrs. Matthews and Cook waited. At 7 AM, Cook fell asleep in her chair.

At 8 AM, the doctor came into the waiting room. Mrs. Matthews shook Cook to wake her up.

The doctor removed his mask.

The two women could see what had happened in his eyes.

The doctor said, "I'm sorry. We did everything we could."

Ronald's funeral was held in a big church. 15 members of the Matthews family came. Aunt Irene came. Ronald's dad came, all the way from Kenya. He pushed a copy of a book into the casket. Andy the tutor came. People said that Ronald looked nice in the casket, like he was sleeping. Mary Margaret, Ann and Max, and Jan came. They sat in the back with their parents. Ann cried all through the service. Max wiped away tears but pretended it was just because of his allergies. The famous TV reporter came and two representatives of the space program. The mayor of Chicago sent one of his aides. Lots of people sent flowers. Everyone agreed it was a miracle that Ronald had lived as long as he did.

After the funeral, Max told anyone who asked him he didn't want to talk about Ronald. For a long time, he had dreams about Ronald. In Max's dream, he would be someplace public, like at school or in a store. Lots of people. And then he would see Ronald. Ronald would just be right there. Max would approach Ronald and whisper, "Hey, man, how can you be here? You shouldn't be here! You're dead, man." And Ronald would put his finger to his lips and say, "Shhh. Don't tell anybody."

Ann came to school with red eyes for several days. She drew a picture of Ronald, folded it up, and kept it in her purse. Sometimes, in study hall, she unfolded the picture and touched it with her fingers.

Ronald's handwritten stories about Insect Boy circulated around the neighborhood. Kids read them until they fell to pieces.

CHAPTER 33: THE POSTHUMOUS LIFE OF THE INSECT BOY STORIES

It turned out that Ronald had left behind copies of his stories. Cook and Mrs. Matthews found a whole folder of them in Ronald's room. Ronald's mother saved them. She told Cook it just felt wrong to throw them away, even if they were sort of creepy.

Mrs. Matthews kept the handwritten stories in her office. She kept them in a cardboard box with a black ribbon around it. Sometimes when she did not feel like working on a case, she would think about Ronald and pull out the box. She would open it and read one of the stories. Sometimes she got tears in her eyes as she read. When she read a story, it was almost like hearing Ronald's voice. When she finished reading the story, she would put it back in the box with the others.

One day Mrs. Matthews asked her secretary if she knew any publishers. The secretary said she didn't. She would have been happy to look up the names and addresses of publishers for Mrs. Matthews, but they were right in the middle of a big case involving a bank robbery. By the time that case ended, the two women had forgotten all about the idea of getting the stories published.

When Mrs. Matthews died many years later (of natural causes; the funeral was attended by all the best criminals in Chicago), her possessions went to her favorite niece Margo Robinson. Margo found the box of stories when she was cleaning out her aunt's house.

Margo read one of Ronald's stories, but she did not like insects. The handwriting on the stories had grown faint but was still legible. For safety's sake, Margo gave the stories to a typist and had them typed up. She thought maybe when her little boy Davie, who was only 6, got a bit older, she would read the stories to him. She liked to read him stories, and he loved the scary kind. Unfortunately, Margo put the stories on a shelf in a closet and forgot all about them.

When Margo's boy Davie was twelve years old and his mother was not in the house, Davie discovered the box of stories his mother had put on a shelf in the closet. It was December, and he was investigating all the nooks and crannies of the house just in case his mom had hidden any presents for him. He sat down on the floor and read the first story. He was going to read just one story, but he ended up carrying the entire box to his room. That night, he stayed up late in his room and read the stories. All of them. He loved the stories about insects so much that for several weeks he told all his friends that, when he grew up, he was going to be an entomologist. He said by the time he was an adult, probably the scientists would have invented a shrink ray. If that happened, he planned to become the first entomologist to have himself shrunk just so he could study the lifestyles of insects up close and personal.

In fact, when Davie grew up, he became a dentist. By then, he had forgotten all about the box of stories.

Years later, one of the dentist's daughters, a 13-year-old girl named Lisa, discovered the box of stories in the attic of her grandmother's house. Like her father, she loved Ronald's stories, but she did not develop a desire to become an entomologist. Nor did she believe it was very likely scientists would ever invent a shrink ray.

Lisa thought it was a pity that the stories had never been published. Maybe she could get them published. That would be pretty cool. With her dad's permission, Lisa started writing letters to publishers. Unfortunately, the publishers—the few who answered her letters—told her they did not think there was any market for stories about talking insects, especially since the author who wrote the stories had been dead for many years.

When Lisa was 19 years old, she attended a small university in a state not too far from Chicago. She had an elderly professor whom she liked, even if he was a bit long-winded and overly fond of old poetry.

One day, she carried the box of Ronald's stories to the professor's office and plumped it down on top of his desk.

She said, "You write books, don't you? Aren't you a published author?"

The professor admitted that he had in fact written a few books, though he hoped she would not hold that against him. He was the kind of professor who said things like that.

Lisa said the box contained stories written by one of her ancestors, a kid named Ronald who had died young.

The professor said, "Oh dear, I am sorry for your loss."

Lisa said it wasn't that much of a loss in her case because the boy had died before she was even born.

"The stories are about talking insects. You know, like spiders and ants and what not, and they talk."

The professor wondered if the talking insects ever said anything interesting. He said he felt the market for stories like that might be greater if the insects at least had interesting things to say.

Lisa said her ancestor, the boy who wrote the stories, had been somewhat famous.

"They called him the Boy Who Could Not Be Touched. He was allergic to … well, to practically everything, I guess. For his whole entire life, he lived inside a hermetically sealed room. There were articles about him in big city newspapers and everything."

The professor said that boy sounded familiar, but he seemed to recall the poor kid lived in a bubble.

"Wasn't there a movie about him?"

Lisa said, "I looked it up. There was a movie about a different kid who was allergic to everything. In fact, there were two movies about this other kid. His name was David Vetter. The first one was made in 1976 and starred John Travolta. It was called *The Boy in the Plastic Bubble*. The second one was made in 2001 and starred Jake Gyllenal. That one was called *Bubble Boy*." Lisa told the professor that, because of these movies, the bubble boy was way more famous than her ancestor.

"I mean, my ancestor just lived in a room. Who cares about a boy who lived in a room? Everyone lives in a room."

The professor said he did not know much about the market for stories about talking insects or boys who spend their entire lives stuck in a room, but he would check into it. He thought the fact the author had died young might help a bit, give the stories a sort of romantic glamor. He was the kind of professor who said things like that.

"These stories aren't very romantic if you ask me," Lisa said. "They're creepy and funny and sad, sometimes all at the same time. I think kids would like them. Some kids would."

One day, a month later, the professor asked Lisa to stop by his office. When she did, he told her he had discovered there was a publisher in England that ran an enterprise called The Ginger Fyre Press.

"One of their claims to fame is that sometimes they publish books written by children. Their slogan is, 'Stories written by kids, for kids!'"

He said if she liked, he could contact that publisher on her behalf.

He said, "Nothing ventured, nothing gained."

"Go for it," Lisa said.

The professor talked to the publisher, and the publisher read Ronald's stories. She called the professor when she finished and asked, "So who owns these stories exactly?"

The professor said it wasn't easy to say, possibly a dentist, or perhaps the mother of the dentist.

"The boy who wrote them is deceased, I am afraid."

This sort of thing went on for a long time. The professor retired and had time on his hands. He told the publisher maybe he would take a stab at telling the whole story of Ronald.

"We could publish Ronald's stories and the story of Ronald, all in one book."

"Let's give it a shot," the publisher said.

And in due course, that is exactly what they did.

The End

www.ingramcontent.com/pod-product-compliance
Lightning Source LLC
Chambersburg PA
CBHW040524170726

48295CB00012B/330

9 781914 071898